DJ Zom-B

& The Ungrateful Dead

Vinnie Penn

ISBN
0-9824777-2-4 (10 digit)
978-0-9824777-2-4 (13 digit)

Library of Congress Catalog Number: 2011923475

First Edition

Printed in the United States of America
Published by 23 House Publishing
SAN 299-8084
www.23house.com

Table of Contents

Acknowledgments

Mitchel from 23House, for going out on such a limb; Dave Dorman, whose incredible artwork graces the cover, and who took the book to the next level the second he said yes; Denise Dorman; Sal Melchiore, for the reference material and unwavering support; Paul Bass/New Haven *Independent* for the back cover photo; Mike Opelka and Charlie Athanas; LA Banks; Tom "Ivan" Ivanovich and Carl Osgood; and two amazing bands who couldn't be more polar opposite: *Deer Tick* and *Kirby Krackle*.

For my Stella and Luke,
who did the homework with me.

Soon I may die
Yes one day I will die
I'll get eaten by the rust
You cremate and breathe the dust
And I'll weaken your lungs
And I'll bite off your tongue.

"Christ Jesus"
Deer Tick

Prologue:
The Date — *Next Week*

Mercedes had the entire club in the palms of her tiny hands, which were presently wrapped around a microphone. She cooed her new single, the title track from her new album *Love U 2 Pieces*. Her deejay was working the sample of Janis Joplin's *Piece of my Heart* with two fingers, with the precision as if he was deactivating a bomb. More than half his body was covered in ink, reds and yellows reaching up his forearms, striving for shoulder.

This was the second *Mercedes* record in a two-record deal, and she was lucky she even got it. She'd had one hit off her first CD, a catchy, thumping, nightclub favorite, *Random*. But the follow-up single tanked. For a 21-year-old she already felt like the industry chewed her up, spit her out, and dozens of Italian shoe-covered feet had stomped all over her.

Her father was Italian (he wanted her to be named Aida, after the opera) and her mother Puerto Rican (mom

1

won—in court, too), and the mixture resulted in long black incorrigible curls framing the delicate features of her face, enviable olive skin presently buried in bad club lighting.

Good thing, though, as Mercedes hasn't slept in days. Anxiety will keep the artist up at night much more certainly than cocaine. Plus, she believed blow was for losers, and even turned down her first record deal offer because the guy from the label had offered her a line.

She was decked out in skintight black and silver, a sliver of her own ink riding down the inside of her forearm, a lone vine with some tiny buds. She had on thigh-high boots and enough makeup to slip on should she really work up a sweat. Her eyebrows were thick and sculpted, like islands on the map that was her face. She was beautiful but had long since forgotten that, and the folks at the far end of the nightclub might not even be aware of it themselves.

The moment for the high note came. She approached it tentatively, breathing techniques incorporated, slow and building. Just as she was about to hit it—"going for it" as it were—there was the sound of glass shattering above the din of the music.

Perfect. Her moment ruined by a shitty waitress.

Mercedes rolled with it, rolling her tongue, changing things up performance-wise, ever the pro. Craning her neck, she sought out the inept waitress, envisioning a clumsy, fast-pitch softball-playing Connecticut big girl. Her eyes scanned the back wall of the South Norwalk club. What she saw instead was what looked like people—customers—being pulled backwards into darkness. It looked as if they were screaming. Instead, it would probably turn out to be just part of some big foam party her people—nay, person—forgot to tell her about.

Mercedes was pissed. She glanced back at Smack, her deejay.

He'd seen that look before, and immediately attempted to lighten the mood. "Shit's getting' crazy in har!" he shouted into his microphone, all piratey. "Say what??"

The crowd responded: "What!?"

"Say what!?"

"What!?"

"SAY WHAT!?"

"WHAT!?"

"Mercedes in the house, say 'Oh yeah...'"

"Oh yeah!"

"Say, 'Oh yeah!'"

"OH YEAH!"

"Wanna get loved to pieces!?" Smack asked, rhetorically of course. Mercedes began bobbing her head to that one. He was getting to her, performing what was, arguably, the most important part of his job—bringing the crowd into her performance. "I said, 'Wanna get loved to PIECES!?'"

But no one answered this second time. Chaos had erupted. People were slipping and falling hard; those who weren't were attempting to climb over the fallen, their movements punctuated by the sound of bones being broken by clomping shoes. Then someone threw something at Smack, or so it seemed. Either way, an object was hurtling towards his head. He ducked just in time, visibly angry. He stopped the music.

"Fuck this. Fuck this! Uptight Connecticut chumps,"

3

he began, Mercedes slumped before him. His eyes scanned the floor surrounding his turntable, seeking out the plastic beer bottle, or whatever it was that had been thrown at him. "You got no heart. You got no soul. That's the stuff music is made of, heart and soul. Damn, y'all don't even got no decency. No common sense. That's what's wrong with the world. Use your heads, Connecticut. Show some respect."

He stopped just then, even while Mercedes was eyeing him woefully, both touched and torn by his diatribe. But Smack had found what had been flung in his general direction and picked it up to throw it back. It was tricky, slipping out of his hand, like it was alive, a wiggling newborn animal.

"Throw shit at me and I'll throw it right..."

He raised it up, but squeezed too hard and it slipped out of his hand and landed with a thud onto his console. It was a human heart.

"It's getting kinda lonely out here by myself
Food's running low
There's dust on the shelf
But at least I have the voices arguing in my head
which is much better than being undead."

"Zombie Apocalypse"
Kirby Krackle

Chapter 1:
The Day Before Tomorrow

I once stayed awake for five straight days. I was in Los Angeles, at the start of my radio career, and scored some blow. Only it wasn't blow, it was some shit those Left Coast la-la lunatics call crank, and sleep went the way of appetite, rational thought, and erectile function. I remember asking an extra from a Bon Jovi video what day it was and she answered, "The day before tomorrow."

Back then we were locked up in a tiny apartment, looking like vampires, blood on our nostrils as opposed to the tips of our teeth.

Now I was holed up in another tiny apartment in Connecticut, and a vampire would be a sight for sore eyes... because presently, all that was out there were zombies. I didn't know how many days it had been going on—I'd lost count. It's the day before tomorrow, is what it is. Tomorrow the sun will rise, and that would fry an army of vampires. But zombies? They don't even sweat.

3

I had been watching the news. Well, more specifically an anchor I find attractive and who I thought I might be able to sidle up to thanks to my return to the airwaves about a year ago—even if it is in the Adult Contemporary format. She and her co-anchor were live at a pub where a fire had broken out. Next thing I know zombies are pulling him apart like he's a lobster and I'm watching them pick at his meat, feverishly, and for a good minute before the Action News camera drops to the ground. I'm assuming the cameraman ran for the hills, or was dessert.

I immediately made a few phone calls, mostly to stoned married friends who thought I was preparing material to jut in between a Richard Marx tune and a Bryan Adams cut, promptly laughing me off, as if I am allowed to talk about anything other than reality television voting results on my "new morning show."

"That's funny stuff," one said.

"*War of the Worlds* returns," said another.

Less than half an hour later I overheard my neighbor and his new girlfriend being gorged on—a veritable orchestra of screaming, snapping, and lip-smacking.

Mourning show is more like it.

I went to call my friends back but the landline was dead. Used my cell phone, got one on the line.

"Will you stop with this shit?" he said. "Me and the Missus are getting busy." I heard her voice, muffled, giggling; "Don't tell him!" She sounded just under the phone. Then I heard a loud crash. I shouted his name. It was the last thing he heard—me shouting his name.

I listened to the whole thing, a sorta telephone rubbernecking. I listened to my friend being eaten alive.

* * * * *

Fetal position, corner; this is me, this is now. I am a snail, human escargot for the undead. I await the clanging of their dinner bell. Have been for two, maybe three, even four days. Damned if I know.

But, they don't come. They haven't come, not yet, and there is a creeping sense of potential survival. I do not wish to take them on, nor do I wish to somehow skirt their uprising, ultimately returning to the airwaves with some Zombie Top 20 Countdown show in tow, theme song by The Hooters, and AC/DC's *Highway to Hell* the perennial number one. I just want to live. And this ain't livin'.

I sneak a peek out my window. The streets are empty, ragged shirts and pants strewn about, some cars looking meticulous, beckoning. "Hotwire me," they say. But I can't. I could have bought a hot car in my day but could never steal my own; I bought the drugs but never sold them, or cut them, or poured them into little baggies. I am a consumer in the midst of a mass consumption.

I really don't know what to do. I haven't heard so much as a peep—outside of the voices in my head—in close to a day, maybe two. It's all maybes. The days are maybes. If anyone else in the entire complex is alive is a maybe. My survival is a maybe. I feel like the second I decide to step outside this overpriced shit apartment to seek out any other survivors, I'll be picked off, a chicken wing at the zombie happy hour. Lukewarm.

That's my name, by the way: Luke. Last name Zombulli. On the air I went by DJ Zom-B. How's that for irony? Even got a big "Z" tattooed on my neck. Everyone makes Zorro jokes. It's a little too big, black, and there are red "drops of blood" falling from it.

I am not preoccupied with *how* this happened. Not even *why*. I was the same way when I was doing my old, far more successful and better-paying morning show on the morning of 9/11. Phone calls came pouring in, nameless, faceless listeners suddenly well versed in overseas activity, spouting philosophy, ideology, and names I'd never heard before. Saddam Hussein. Osama Bin Laden. I was a Top 40 jock far more used to names like Salma Hayek and Mary-Kate Olsen. They had the how's, the why's...and the who's. I was more concerned with the "What now?"

Just like now.

There is a surge of energy. Synapses fire. I am suddenly tearing through the closet, tearing at clothes, tearing up. Then I cut myself. If you read that back you'd think I was a supermodel.

But I wanted blood, even though a part of me thought I just might be turning myself into chum; my thought, irrational as it may be—is to get out there, see what's what, and to do so I have to be prepared for the possible zombie flood. Rather than be drowned, my idea is to body surf, and to do that I have to look like one, move like one, even think like one. The blood can only help, in a "costume" capacity, but what if drawing my own blood only succeeds in tantalizing their taste buds?

Alas, it is too late, the blood congealing, drying, latching onto the myriad coarse hairs on the forearm of my Italian-American arm. The infliction felt good, the lingering sting more so. Deserved even.

And that "deserved" compels me to tell you a bit about myself:

You see, as a radio "personality," a local celebrity of sorts, I am equal parts self-absorbed and self-loathing. Comes with the gig, really. A benefit not unlike dental.

I got into radio just out of high school, at a rock station in New Haven, circa '89. Sporting a mullet, shark tooth earring, and a knowledge of all things hair band, I was the perfect foil for the then-morning team, Chico & The Boner (real names Frank DeLucia and Gary Tagliatti). It was also the perfect side gig for a guitarist whose band was slowly but surely making a name for itself.

"Gangbusters" was cracking New York already, for Christ's sake, inasmuch as Long Island is considered New York. Hey, we'd gotten a Village Voice mention.

Even so, radio was happening faster for me as a foil than a guy with a Fender.

This did not bode well on occasion for Chico & The Boner, the latter of whom I once throttled at a radio station event—"remotes" we in the biz call them. He took a potshot at my seemingly stalled music career and I choked him down to the puke, piss and spilt drink-ridden floors of the bar.

Yep, I have anger issues. Or, *had* anger issues. It got me suspended from high school many a time, although this was the day and age before New Age words like anger issues, "timeouts," and passive aggression. This was pre-Ritalin, motherfuckers. There was nothing passive about aggression, and it got your transcript rubberstamped. You were labeled a punk, not the genteel "problematic."

By the time my gig on the radio show was taking off, so to speak, I had convinced myself I had it all in check: the short temper, shorter wick, non-existent patience. (I was particularly foul at supermarkets; one particular price check, thanks to an inept, devoid-of-personality cashier, took the length of *Dances with Wolves,* and resulted in some of my most venomous vitriol to date. Not pretty.)

Thankfully, Boner never mentioned the fact that I strangled him at a decidedly un-Happy Hour, but my days on his morning show were still numbered.

I was a tool tooling around town in a Chevy Camaro whose recurring phone calls into said radio show as a character I created called "Rad Tad" (the *epitome* of passive aggressive, as I lambasted hipsters by playing one, with the catch phrase, "Aren't I just the raddest, baddest loser?") ultimately gave way to third billing, then co-hosting duties when Boner decided he *did* have a bone to pick with Chico, and then an offer from the Top 40 station across town came my way with a six figure salary attached, plus a car deal.

Bye, bye anger.

Or so I thought.

During my semi-successful run I went from 180 lbs., long hair *and* a long line of girlfriends, and a basement-cum-bachelor pad in my parent's house, to 210 lbs., a fiancé, and my own home—only to eventually become the 220 lb. studio apartment dweller on a bicycle with a shaved head presently wounding himself either in a half-baked attempt to walk among the undead, or more than likely to serve myself to them.

Uncertainty about one's true intentions is also counted among the benefits of the radio host, this one not unlike, say, vision.

The only concert tee I have the heart to sacrifice is a Smashing Pumpkins one, thumbing the frayed, softened cotton of my Bon Jovi *New Jersey* tee as if it is a "Dear John" letter and me some heartbroken soldier awash in nostalgia. Ah, to go back to that night, that concert, that unconscionable rendition of *Shout* as an encore, even if *Bad Medicine* led into it; my hand woven into my date's, sweat permeating the very shirt I hold in it now, it perhaps having never even been laundered, the car sex punctuating the evening like an exclamation point at the end of a most awesome sentence.

Now I just wonder if she's even still alive.

My parents, sadly, both died during my last round of unemployment, which came thanks to both a hair-brained stunt I was against in the first place and some on-air monologues that blurred the line between Top 40 and talk radio. I was railing against my Catholic upbringing, local politics, and taking calls on things like fate versus free will rather than Britney Spears versus Christina Aguilera.

Furthermore, radio unemployment can be like dog years. Two months after being fired from my increasingly long and rage-fueled tirades and my, let's just say "heated," reaction to the aforementioned stunt, I began anger management classes (court-ordered) and my dad passed from lung cancer. What's worse, the radio stunt I was against doing in the first place resulted in something horrible and if I had just been vocal there, instead of everywhere else, it might not have happened. It was a stupid, tired (two words wholly applicable to yours truly) stunt, and entirely unsafe. I said nothing, ever—merely rolled my eyes during the countless promotional meetings leading up to it. I was the scapegoat in a radio stunt gone awry—that was my dad's last snapshot of me, which caused even more anger.

Tragically, he still had hope in his eyes during his brief Hospice stay, and not for himself but for me. He figured major market offers loomed, my recent break-up only a speed bump, and that my shaved head was a fashion choice and not because washing it had become an annoyance. The old man, I suspect, liked my anger, though he never said as much.

Two years after that my mother passed from pancreatic cancer. She still had hope in her eyes, not for me but for herself. Her death was a blow from which I would not recover.

The upside? Anger management was no longer necessary; I was defeated, and remain so.

My non-ballyhooed return to Connecticut airwaves, on the adult contemporary station that effectively castrated my personae, came within the next year. Cancer had ravaged them both, consumed them. Or, moreover, the chemo did. I watched them writhe in agony, eyes askew, mumbling incoherently. I held each of their hands until they both went limp.

To be honest, the zombie-out seems preferable.

As I unlatch my lock, "costume" pristine and zombie walk perfected, I finally digest the fact that I've heard naught for an eternity; I stopped pressing my ear to my walls and to the floor eons ago. I pause to wonder if I am finally the "last man on earth" that so many ladies had mentioned to me in my life.

There was nothing much to see from my peephole all this time. A blood splatter on the door directly across from me, Apartment 6. Or was it merely graffiti? I'm amazed at my detachment.

I step out into the hall and the silence gives me a

disconcerting hug. Floorboards creak, in that B-movie way. I want to check on the neighbors, a couple dabbling in cohabitation to "see how it feels." Those were his words; hers were "stepping stone." Maybe it's the same thing. Maybe it's lost in translation. But I think better of doing so, especially as I recall that I heard them actually being eaten.

"Down the stairs," I hear. "Out the door." It's me. Talking to me.

But when I look down the stairs I see said neighbor—or what's left of him anyway—strewn about the foyer: torso on the floor mat, legs on the stairs, guts like silly string. Oh, and head nowhere to be found. His name was Bill. Never really liked him, and his live-in girlfriend was cute in a "wing-man" capacity, but still, seeing him dissected like this is vomit-inducing. So I do. Everywhere.

The stench is evidently a zombie calling card. They pour out of an apartment on the bottom floor, faces covered in what looks like Spaghettio's yet probably isn't, but maybe is, and I somehow manage to launch into performance mode: *Groan, drag foot, drool, repeat. Groan, drag foot, drool, repeat.*

Freaks actually buy it.

Next thing ya know I'm walking among them, out of Home Sweet Home and into the street, and I can't help wondering where the Vincent Price voiceover is at. Aw, that's just the '80s/DJ guy in me talking.

I make a conscious effort to keep my heart steady, as if there was some Zombie Survival Guide that I had committed to memory, the very guy who could tune a stewardess' "what to do in case of emergency" dissertation out with the best of them.

11

There's five or six zombies. I avoid eye contact, especially with the one whose eye is actually hanging out of the socket. Their odor verges on unbearable. If not for being outside and sucking in the air I'd definitely puke. Again. I think that that's probably a milkshake to these things and laugh a little; this catches the attention of the one closest to me, what was once a female. I hear her grunt and when she twists her neck to look at me, its sound like someone crumpling up a McDonald's bag.

Suddenly my heartbeat seems inordinately loud.

Boom.

I feel a bead of sweat form on my forehead.

BOOM.

It triples in size.

BOOM!

Starts racing down the size of my face.

I swear Zombette can either hear the heartbeat or smells the salt in my perspiration. The jig is up.

Fortuitously, a mailman hanging out of his crashed mail truck picks the worst timing imaginable to regain consciousness and it's like the horn on a lunch truck is honked. They converge upon all his human hamburger glory.

Zombette still appears acutely aware of my disguise so I am left to swoop in alongside them. The mailman's cries are a combination of delirium and gut-wrenching pain, and he's hitting a high note that is reminiscent of a time I saw Mariah Carey perform at the honoring of a record label exec. One zombie tears the mailman's chest open like it's a Christmas present. There is an explosion of intestine, vein, lung, and heart. The subsequent gurgling sound is either his innards spilling forth, them feasting, or both simultaneously. It's a feeding frenzy and as someone trying to blend I do the only thing one can do in this situation.

I hop into the driver side of his truck, turn the key in the ignition, and punch it.

Chapter 2:
Urban Miffed

Getting situated in the mail truck isn't easy. They don't exactly stock these suckers with a state-of-the-art stereo system, and photos of ugly children are flying at me from off of the dashboard and from beneath the visor I immediately pull down to block the blinding sunlight; the former is noticed because I wanted to put on the radio and hopefully hear a newscast on all things zombie, and the latter confirms that sunlight does not do the same to zombies as it does to vampires. I don't even think a zombie can get a sunburn.

I lost power in my apartment the second all hell broke loose. I can only imagine the catalyst. Fire in the basement? The undead feasting on wiring like its licorice whips? Is the power out statewide?

Who knows and who cares...I'm driving a fucking mail truck and being behind the wheel on the right side of a vehicle doesn't feel right at all, like jerking off with my

15

left hand.

I spent a good portion of that long first night wondering what other things I dismissed as the product of Poe's imagination as a child might be true, the whimsy of a fanciful poet, or even the weary ramblings of a father looking to scare my nine-year-old self to sleep.

The list was endless as the night itself.

Vampires.

Werewolves.

Mummies rising from tombs, tattered bandages like bandannas on Steven Tyler's mike stand.

Santa Claus.

Easter Bunny.

Tooth Fairy.

Was the urban myth itself an urban myth? In which case the story about my babysitter and the hot dog... well, never mind.

* * * * *

The road stretches before me, front doors to homes flung open, as if everyone were airing their house out, one big collective venting. I imagine the blood splattered on the walls inside all of the homes, the ghosts of Christmases past that lurk the tragedy-ridden hallways and living rooms, and think of who just might remain, who I do not have the nerve to seek out, to potentially save. Is this, in fact, my chance at righting the wrong of that stupid radio contest?

I don't know where I'm going. But there's more than a half-tank of gas and I figure just keep on driving; drive 'til I can't drive anymore, and then...drive some more.

Could this be confined to Connecticut? Contained even? I look up into the sky, seeking out a helicopter or jet. The clouds move slowly, lethargic and meandering, like we all got to do for so long. Not so much as a bird.

All I get is a zombie on the hood.

I don't know if I hit him or if he dropped from a tree, to be honest. I'm going with the hitting him scenario, as, from what I've seen, they don't appear to be adept tree-climbers. By the time I'm swerving the mail truck to and fro in an effort to shake him from the hood his fists are already through the windshield, bugs dug into the flesh of the truck, parasite by the dashboard lights.

His grunts annoy me more than terrify me, reminiscent of a drunken uncle who plagued our holiday meals growing up, his recollections of the three wars he served in too much to bear, the bourbon too tempting to pass up. He'd regale us with tales of bloodshed and servitude over manicotti and be passed out and muttering by the time the pastries hit the table.

In all the swerving I feel something drop out of the pocket of my torn hoodie—it's my cell phone; my eyes bulge upon seeing it. It had died but now I could charge it, and lo and behold, there is a charger in the very vehicle I am driving. I fumble for the phone with one hand, steer with the other. Zombie on the hood ain't having any of this, though, haphazardly digging its way towards me, the windshield and fiberglass like fresh soil, just another grave to dig out of. When he finally grabs hold of one of my arms I panic, doing the zombie algebra:

a scratch that draws blood =
slow transformation to zombie myself

17

My knee-jerk reaction is to cram my cell phone, my all-important I-Pad, into this creature's eye. The sound is repugnant. What's worse, he barely registers what appears to only be a minor discomfort. His face literally swallows the phone.

I decide to slam on the brakes, which thrusts him off the hood and into the road before me. Then run him over. Then reverse, drive, run him over a second time. As I race away I see him rise in the rearview mirror, none the worse for wear.

This is when I hit two more.

Thanks to the shattered windshield left behind by my first zombie hit-and-run they are both practically inside the truck in no time. I have no choice but to intentionally drive into a telephone pole, which effectively separates their upper halves from their lower halves. It also destroys the vehicle.

I stagger away from the wreckage, checking myself for blood, for scratches in particular. My crash course in Romero, an early '90's, hash-fuelled long weekend of ramen noodles and zombie movies, leaves me thinking a mere scratch from the undead could result in a prolonged transformation into same. Wobbly and distracted, I pat myself up and down my forearms, and across my face and forehead. Free and clear.

My eyes begin to trace the fallen phone lines, immense wiring akin to a yellow brick road of its own. I begin to follow it, and the sound of the recently severed zombies echo in the background, the creatures dragging their upper halves slowly – but surely – in my general direction.

I once got lost at the supermarket as a kid. My mother was torn between two tampons, feeling like a fool, and I just wandered. I couldn't have been more than five years old at the time.

Realizing that I was lost, that instant, the dawning on me that I could not find my way back, that all of these shuffling, towering strangers were the very ones I'd been repeatedly warned to accept nothing from, say nothing to, avoid at all costs, was suffocating. There wasn't a kind face among them, and the ones attempting to convey kindness, with their toothy suburban smiles, were scarier than the stoic.

The store became instantly, fantastically loud, but inaudible, indecipherable, voice upon voice, the announcements being made being the worst offender. (My name was one of the announcements, but irrationality prevented me from registering it.) I began to shrink. I did not cower, but I shrank. People peered down at me, hanging trees, and they all seemed sinister. Perhaps my parents—God rest their souls, or damn them—drilled this thought process into me, but paranoia and panic reigned. They were plodding, plotting zombies to me—no more and no less.

When one man bent his knees and gingerly placed a hand on my shoulder, softly inquiring if I was lost I screamed as if Satan himself had just made his presence known. He disappeared into the checkout crowd, a look of either perplexity or predatory etched upon his face, and I still see it to this day.

When my mother grabbed my arm, jerking me towards her waiting hugs and kisses—and reprimand—I jostled as if a stranger, a predator, a ZOMBIE had grabbed me. She

19

never registered my fear, my borderline urination, instead choosing to reiterate her time-honored "don't wander" dissertation, the "how many times..." end being heavily leaned on.

Sometimes wandering is the only option.

Chapter 3:
United Fates

Following the fallen telephone cables feels like the right thing to do until I ultimately, inevitably wonder why it feels that way. Where do I think it is leading me? Why does it seem appropriate? Moments of crisis reveal to the victim just how unprepared, how unskilled, how supremely vulnerable he or she truly is. I swallow this like the bitterest of pills. I am as unskilled a survivalist as my pre-Boy Scout (Webelos, if I recall) training suggested I would be. The compass was no different than a Rubik's Cube then, the reading of the sun's position in the sky as oblique as geometry.

Yet here I am, real world crashing down—or zombie world, rather—and my Den Leader's premonitions prove dismayingly on target. I am adrift, floating and awaiting assistance. Sadly, none appears to be coming.

Then it dawns on me: the radio station. *A* radio station.

There's a small internet station not far from here, the owner a fallen sales demagogue from Clear Channel's heyday, an entrepreneur who saw a trend coming a mile away but not the fact that the major league industry players would too, plopping all of their popular radio stations on-line as well. Still, it has a presence, an underground community if not thriving then surely humming along, nourished by the local band scene (which any major radio station in a community will by and large avoid like the plague) and ticket giveaways to shows at local venues that...well...can't give 'em away.

Many of my former contemporaries, guys and gals who found themselves nudged out of an ever-shrinking industry, collateral damage in a Seacrest-ed world, turned up at this online-only radio station, schlepping either their questionable talent behind the mike or sales acumen on an unsuspecting, uninformed, mostly broke advertising community.

Their "studio," for lack of a better word, is tiny and moderately depressing, and worse, storefront and central to the art district; it can right now only be a ghost town or awaiting a lone rider. A high plains drifter.

That'd be me.

Aside from all this preamble, it is the closest and first place I can think of, as my "plan of escape/attack" is about as well-calculated as the marketing campaign for this artist named Mercedes' last record, *Love U 2 Pieces*. She's cute and all—reverb and synth in overdrive—and probably dead too, but her career was on life support anyway. She should be glad some undead accountant pulled the plug. We had words on the air once. She was an E! reality show laying in wait.

These digressions are mildly amusing—to me anyway. As terrified as I am, as much as I totally get that this is some heavy shit, a potential worldwide apocalypse (unconfirmed at this point; it still may be confined to either this state or, at the very least, the Northeast), my ability—or the human ability—to avert one's attention to minutia, is obviously pure defense mechanism. We are thrust into a previously unimaginable situation and our inner dialogue sustains us, narrating in an intentionally pseudo-philosophical yet comedic manner our final minutes/hours/days. I'll take days.

In the distance I see the storefront, the radio station strategically placed amidst all the retail, as if the commerce would or could simply spill over, onto the airwaves and into the pockets of the account executive(s). There are power lines down everywhere but I cannot gauge if satellite ones are among them, and discerning if there is some sort of electromagnetic pulse is also beyond me. Hell, that could be exactly what caused all of this. My producer, the radio station technicians and engineers, they tried the best that they could to teach me the simplicity of "powering up" throughout my questionable "career," but damned if I learned a thing. As I now stare certain death in the face, I wonder if I ever truly learned a thing. About anything at all.

I am fuelled by a fear/adrenaline hybrid, moving at a rapid fire pace despite being starved and bloodied and bruised and disoriented. All I see is the radio station in the distance, my focus there, like it used to be on a girl at a bar as last call was bellowed.

The streets are empty, and from what I have seen thus far, the many movies and/or short stories dedicated to zombie mythology are, excuse the pun, *dead on*. They don't move fast at all, plus seem incapable of hiding, waiting for the precise moment to emerge from behind a dumpster or some equivalent, and attack. Brain power and running is beyond them. You'd think that'd make for one hell of an easy adversary to elude.

Maybe. File me under *maybe* at the moment.

* * * * *

Another digression: Have you ever gone house hunting? The owners are gone—out killing time, praying their negligence won't prevent a sale, hoping the fist-holes in the walls look like hammers that missed the nail, not the domestic dispute road kill they really are—and you step down into the basement and it's silent in a way that's eerie. You immediately wonder about mice, think you have enough of a trained eye to spot some trace, like mouse droppings look decidedly different than bits of soil shaken from beneath a shoe. There is an order in the disorder. You survey the area, and just when you turn you think you hear a noise, and turn back quickly, certain you will catch some vermin presuming that they can best you. You don't, of course, but you think about said vermin the entire way home, compartmentalizing the realtor's sales pitch.

This is Earth. Today. Or, at the very least, New Haven.

The storefronts are creepily silent, like one grand trap. However, zombies are incapable of punking, although one or two of them looked and moved a little like Ashton Kutcher. I met him once at a *Maxim* magazine red carpet event. He gave very funny quotes and then the exact same ones to the next radio personality and on down the line. Then the next celebrity came, gave me funny quotes, and the same to the radio guy next to me and so forth. Fairly zombie-like, in retrospect.

Only one of the stores sports a smashed front window and I notice that the shattered glass is not on the sidewalk but, instead, on the inside of the store, meaning whatever broke through it went from the outside in, as opposed to the inside out. God bless every "CSI" show, especially the one with David Caruso. Come to think of it, one of the zombies looked like him, too.

I turn the knob on the front door of the radio station, which is directly next door, and while I should probably avoid all together, especially in light of my recent observation, what else am I to do, where am I to go? I don't have the slightest idea.

The door is unlocked. I step inside and immediately hear a shotgun being cocked. I turn and see it aimed right at me.

"DJ Zom-B. As I live and breathe," the man holding it says.

I recognize him but the name does not come. He is disheveled, always disheveled, shirt as un-tucked as it is never-been-ironed, his neck eating his head. Looks older than me but is probably younger. "Hey...d-dude," I stammer. "Leaving the door unlocked? Not too smart."

"Why? Zombies knock?" he fires back, figuratively, thankfully, laughing and placing the firearm down. "Saw four gang-bangers gutted in the back alley two days ago. Motherfuckers were pulled inside fucking out, guns and knives still in their hands, clenched tight. And a deejay manages to stay alive. Go figure."

"Yeah, well, cowering is key," I tell him. "What was your name again?"

"Same as the last five times you asked, at the last five radio station events I worked sound at for you." He lights up what's left of a cigarette, a skinny little brown one. "Ivan."

"Right. We...safe here or what?"

"We are until I run out of ammo."

"And the last time you saw a...um..."

"Doornail?"

"Huh?"

"That's what I call 'em," Ivan informs me. "They're dead as doornails, right? You've heard that saying."

I nod. Of course, technically, they're undead, but I've never been one to stop a catch phrase that's got momentum going for it. "Actually, I meant one of us. Ya know, a human."

He pauses to think about this. Tosses what's left of his cigarette down, stubs it out with a sizable work-boot. "Heard one a day or so ago."

"You go out there?" I ask.

"An' what...? Play hero? Waste ammo?"

"I wouldn't regard it as wasting..." I begin, taken aback at my self-righteous indignation, something I've only ever unleashed on-air, as hollow then as my enthusiasm regarding a new Sting song.

"S'funny. Gal was screaming 'Omigod, omigod.' Sounded the same as sex." He pauses to further deliberate and, of course, ultimately elaborate. "Sex and death sound the same."

It actually makes sense.

I look around. He has totally set up camp, and with all of the empty food containers, wrappers, etc., and everything else that is in plain sight—batteries, soda cans, magazines, neatly stacked toilet paper rolls, and more—he just might be the one doing the breaking in around here. I look over at the computer; it looks like he's got service, like he's on-line. I walk over cautiously, not wanting to find out what I'm fairly certain I'm about to find out.

"Are you on the air?" I ask.

He shakes his head slowly, no.

"Are you on-line?"

Changes it to a yes.

There is a coloring book-esque map of the United States up on the screen and the Connecticut part, tiny little spec that it is, towering only in the minds of Rhode Islanders, is pulsating—a flashing, throbbing red; doing the same are Nevada and one other state I'd never been able to pick out on a blank map since grade school. Maine is yellow.

"What's the...uh...website you're on here, Ivan?"

"United Fates," he replies calmly. "Dot-com, o'course."

"Of course," I say.

There is a beep just then. Or a blip, rather. I notice that a number in the upper right-hand corner went up simultaneously. It's in the upper thousands and beeps again, and then again.

I squint to read the word beneath the ever-changing number: "Body count-o-meter...?"

"I don't even hear the beeps anymore," Ivan tells me.

This is a lot to take in. I went from days on end curled up in a corner, to thrusting myself onto the streets in a zombie parade, narrowly escaping in a mail truck, and wind up here. I'm staring at a computer screen that has a website dedicated to this gruesome turn of events, tallying up the deaths somehow, while a nonchalant hillbilly of sorts sits in the corner whose plan it is to wait for the zombies to turn up and blow them away with a shotgun until he runs out of ammo. I worried about containment, that this might not be worldwide, or even nationwide, and here I am fairly close to correct; three states apparently have had a surge in the zombie population and are not only being left to their own devices, but Big Brother is cannily watching and generating revenue.

"How can they be finding out?" I ask. "Who's reporting back the...the...deaths?"

"Prob'ly a bunch of kids out there with I-thingys, all in cahoots," replies Ivan. He's not even so much as glancing out the window.

"Or it's all bullshit," I say. "One big panic button being pushed."

"An' what...? The zombies are soldiers or some shit? This is some government-driven population control situation? Fuckers seem to like the taste of flesh and blood if that's the case."

The beeping has become incessant. I move the arrow over to the little speaker icon in the lower corner of the screen and click on mute. "First of all...Ivan," I begin, and I say it in a tone ordinarily reserved for thickheaded radio listeners, as I've never felt comfortable using it face to face, never felt superior enough, but the microphone plus facelessness equals oodles of bravado and confidence, "kudos on such a thought-out conspiracy theory. Mine certainly isn't even a toe in that water.

This...number...might just simply justify our being abandoned. Somebody cranks it up and up and then they can write us off comfortably. Justifiable quarantine."

"You're shittin' me, right? This state's a ghost town!"

"Or so they'd have everyone believe."

I am grasping at straws really, irked by Ivan's insouciance, his apparent need to accept that anything we might even think of doing will be for naught. I look at the laptop again, and think of Block Island. I took up surfing a few summers ago, my anger so not managed, wildly out of control at the time. Popped a Jack Johnson CD in the car stereo and made a break for the Ferry. Next thing you know it was Split Rock Cove for an entire month and I swear it was working. Surfer Zen put Buddhism to shame, and the surfer chicks were the ultimate perk. Buddhist chicks were a drag. Even the teas paled in comparison.

Then, one glorious August morning, sun barely up, there was a good swell and barely any undertow. What there was, however, was an octopus-like seaweed that dragged me into the most jagged rock in the North-East. It tore my leg open and I spent the next two hours cussing out my board like it was a living thing. People were taking pictures with their phones.

"Yeesh," groans Ivan, snapping me out of it, tugging on yet another cigarette but deciding against it, pushing it back into the pack. There are dozens of cartons, color-coordinated, stacked neatly in one corner of the room; if his ammo is in accordance to his smokes he's got a ton of rounds to go. Or smokes like a fiend. "No wonder your ratings suck. Was that supposed to qualify as dramatic delivery? Damn, you were actually pretty good when you were doing Top 40, too. 'Til that stupid obstacle course stunt. Sorry about that, man."

"About bringing it up or what happened because of it?" I fire back. "Never mind. Speaking of radio, are these guys on the air? Is anyone on the air?"

"Not in Connecticut. 'Cuz, um, they're *all dead*." He goes for the smoke now. Gets up even, begins a slow pace, back and forth, more madman than methodical.

"Seventy-five-percent of Connecticut is syndicated, Ivan. You know that. Someone's on. What're they saying?"

"If you're talkin' 'bout some talkin' head in New York then I wouldn't know."

That's exactly what I'm talking. And specifically New York, our Goddamned neighbor, as opposed to Los Angeles, home to the remainder of the syndicated blowhards, both talk and Top 40. Why would this idiot not be trying to get updates?

"Well, I want to," I announce, and lunge for the computer. He grabs my mouse hand, lifts it up into the air, like he's pronouncing me the winner of a prizefight or something.

"You ain't much of a guest," he reprimands, and the sleeve to his long-sleeved shirt drops a bit, revealing some forearm; there's a sizable scratch. I notice it and he notices me noticing it.

Why would he be trying to get updates on the situation, on a zombie army marching the streets? He's gonna be one of 'em in a day or two. Probably less. Much less.

* * * * *

Two helicopters swooped overhead in Fairfield County, ninja-like in their soundlessness, a camouflage blue, perhaps to assist in blending with clouds— nonexistent clouds right now, but no doubt an outstanding suggestion during the blueprint stage. They hovered within an appropriate distance from one another, the pilots in each surveying the streets below, then looking over to one another, and then eyes back down.

Slowly, cautiously, a handful of people emerged from behind upscale boutiques and meticulously landscaped shrubbery. They hooked hands, looking up at the choppers, hope in their eyes. One of them, a man in his late 30's or so, in a seersucker that's seen better days, salt and pepper hair falling in front of his well-chiseled face, raised his hand to remove said hair, a bejeweled watch refracting the sun, catching one pilot's eye. The man waved at the pilot. That chopper nosedived towards them, gracefully, without causing alarm.

"Are you okay?" the pilot inquired via a bullhorn.

The man nodded yes, and his enthusiastic nodding was utterly contagious, everyone else following suit.

"Are there more of you?" the pilot pressed.

The affirmative nodding continued and they signaled for even more Westport folk to join them, Polo-outfitted pub-owning Republicans crowding a street empty less than a minute before. There was approximately two dozen, each one ecstatic.

Until the guns in the choppers were aimed and repeated rounds were fired. They were fish in a bucket. Arms flailed, blood splattered, all in a performance art explosion, one longing for operatic accompaniment. The helicopters then floated further upstate.

One of the pilots looked back, just in time to see six or seven zombies about a block away, yet another dinner bell rung. He was long gone before the feeding began. Oh, what he'd have seen!

By the time the zombies reached the humans just given the Bay of Pigs treatment, which was close to an hour, there were still two or three alive. One man attempted to drag himself away from the scene, but the attempt was futile, even though it was slow-moving zombies on his tail. But his still-beating heart, hot flesh, and other admittedly lukewarm organs rendered him a real catch; while zombies enjoy leftovers, they, not unlike the majority of us, prefer a hot meal.

He was converged upon, zombie teeth inserted into his neck, beneath the rib cage, and upper, inner thigh. His screams were of a pitch that kept the closest birds in their nests, trembling and without song.

Chapter 4:
Dead Air

Neither of us acknowledges the elephant in the room. The zombie elephant, that is. Ivan simply lets go of my arm, tugs the sleeve back over his chewed one, and I go about my scrolling business. I click on a popular New York radio station's website. First thing I see: "Rolling Stones Announce Final Tour!" Scroll down. Second thing I see: "Zombie Outbreak Completely Contained."

He is not exactly at ease with my seeing his lightning bolt-shaped wound, alternately pacing and puffing; we are both lamenting our own private, individual tragedies: his imminent transformation and the utter dissolution of everything he knows and is, and mine, the probably-inevitable feeding frenzy, of which he might be leader. We do not act in accordance to any knowledge of this, instead forging ahead in our own silences, me working internet search engines and him revving his own. Ivan has to be—to a certain extent anyway—either debating doing away with me right here and now since I've deduced his predicament, or wondering if I'm thinking of doing away with him, something I'm loath to do. Instead, I covertly do a breathing exercise taught to me in of my classes.

The minutes plod by, the tiny hourglass on the computer screen symbolic in more ways than zombie scratches, air thick with tension, more than the sterling silver crucifix hanging around his techie neck ever could be.

I want to get to one of the podcasts I frequent, or, at the very least, *had* frequented up until a week or so ago— a talk show host's site whose standing in the business is unparalleled and whose railings about conspiracy are as airtight as a mobster's alibi. Can't get to it.

"Damn!" I shout, simultaneously shoving the computer.

"Steady there, Zom-B!" Ivan says, grabbing the computer, leaning on the 'B' in my tired ol' nom de plume, which right about now reeks of irony the way the air in my old apartment building does of rotting flesh. "What were you lookin' for anyway? Confirmation? Or affirmation?"

I don't even know what he's talking about. How much time does he have anyway? An hour? Two? Twenty-four?

"I wanna go on the air," I tell him instead of answering.

"Deejay egos," he laughs, redirecting the computer. "They know no bounds even in an apocalypse. Betcha Rush roasted a good long time on a spittoon, apple in his mouth."

"Right, Ivan. Getty Lee probably made for a tasty entrée," I shoot back, even while I know it's Limbaugh he's lambasting. In actuality I am in awe of his ability to remain at the ready with a quip even while his soul deteriorates. "I don't wanna go on the air to feed my ego. I wanna go on the air to broadcast to whoever might still be out there. Alive and seeking a way out of this mess. Can you help me do that or not?"

"Only way I can think is by stealing the E.A.S.," he says. I look at him quizzically. "The *Emergency Alert System*." My expression does not change. "Ya know, hijack what they use for an *Amber Alert*."

I am still moderately lost, though not nearly as much. Yet my expression nonetheless compels him to head over to the console, to begin twisting and spinning knobs, pounding on buttons with a forefinger that's the size of a screwdriver and will quite possibly be poking my heart out in no time if I don't find some real allies, and soon.

"C'mon," he keeps saying. "Two, two. C'mon. Two, two."

I, meanwhile, sneak a peak out the window. Oddly, the streets still seem abandoned. This lends credence to his declaration that there's not many humans still alive, but begs the question, "Where are the zombies?"

"C'mon," I hear again. "Ya can't kill the air."

At that exact moment a hand smashes through the window, size of a catcher's mitt, decaying and destructive at the same time. I cannot even begin to describe its shade. Gray seems almost complimentary.

It misses snatching up the back of my head by a quick craning of my neck but begins to feel around the hole it's made, shards of glass sticking out from it yet drawing no blood. I think of the flowers it plucked when blood did flow through it, the hair it tussled and hands it held, swings it pushed and pages of books it turned.

Then, a noise, a clap of thunder, deafening; so loud I close my eyes. Ivan has discharged his weapon. When I open my eyes the zombie's hand is on the floor at my feet, and the arm from which it was blown off is hosing blood all over my face, a thick, dark red liquid that the hand did not indicate could possibly still inhabit the rest of the body.

Another noise, equally thunderous, equally deafening. No eyes closing this time. Nope. I see the zombie's head get blown right off its shoulders.

I remember walking down the halls of my high school day after day, year after year, always feeling as if it was the first time. Even while faces became increasingly familiar—some belonging to guys I'd become friends with and then enemies and then friends again, some belonging to girls I'd become boyfriend to and then not and then some again and others decidedly not, some belonging to guys and girls who were either kept at a distance or chose to—I still maneuvered from stairwell to stairwell, class to class with a sense of marvel; I felt unlike any of them. Neither superior nor inferior—just not like them. They careened towards me, into me, past me, around me, through me—every move predictable, from the high-five to the swatting of a book out of someone's hands to the goosing of a rear-end and on and on.

In gym I hated basketball, but declining the invitation was not an option. RSVP pointless. Your name was barked, whistle shriek immediately following, and next thing you knew you were in these human cages, yearning to break free, ball or not, to blast through the fleshy bars and shackles, even if just to beat your chest and howl.

My moves on the court were decidedly clumsy. They were not born of poetry, nor were mine on the stage born, shorn of method acting, nor mine at the podium fueled by political inclination.

In short, I was a zombie.

Chapter 5:
Kickstart

By the time I realize Ivan is dragging both myself and his laptop out into the back parking lot, the sound of his untied work-boots scuffing concrete, his steps (and belly) indicative of zero treadmill activity, ever, I smell piss. Did I wet myself?

No, it's piss and nicotine. It's Ivan. Has his devolution officially begun?

He is rambling on about satellites being down, but adamant about electricity still being in play. Those are exact words. They play a marching beat on my eardrums, instigate an inner monologue, one loaded with self-deprecation, panic, remorse, wild abandon, and desperation. Bi-polar finally fits.

I have literally survived the past few years of my life on a steady diet of Diazepam and raisin bran. Oh, and the occasional Hydrocodone, thanks to throwing my back out once and having a pharmacist with a daughter who wanted to see every concert in town. That's led to what I wouldn't exactly call an addiction, but perhaps on the rung of the addiction ladder. I am without either medication at this point, even while pharmacies are ripe for the picking right about now; I debate coercing Ivan into a pit-stop but it's not like there is a zombie antidote on the market. Shit, Prozac turns you into one.

"I might be a lame duck but I ain't a sittin' one," he's presently declaring, even though that's exactly what he's been since this all went down—whatever "this" is: satellite, world, God. Yeah, capital 'G.' "We got power. Literally and figuratively," adds Ivan, amidst smoker's wheeze.

I never know what this guy means. I'm also fairly certain he'd say much more compelling stuff on the air than I, which is often the case when it comes to producer versus host. The host has pizzazz, but zero substance; the producer the exact opposite.

He begins using the butt of his shotgun to smash the windows of parked vehicles, obviously having no car of his own. This, of course, is akin to sounding an alarm for zombies, especially since it actually does sound the alarm of several vehicles. Ivan, now, is the nonplussed one, though, alternately smashing and blasting, a symphony of glass and face, glass and face. I can only be dragged along, ever the damsel in distress.

He dismisses one car too quickly, turning to shoot the face off what was probably once a hot girl, judging from the trendy, tiny shirt covered in soot and spit. I spy car keys sitting atop a floor mat.

"Keys!" I shout.

"In!" he replies.

I climb inside the aged Honda Accord, nine years

easy; it wears dents like I do wrinkles from sun damage and stress. Ivan is emptying rounds into the plethora of zombies emerging from who knows where. (I'd say God knows where, but He can surely know nothing of these creatures. Right?)

Then, the lummox does the unthinkable. "Pop the trunk!" he commands, as he simultaneously tosses me his buck knife and rushes back towards the internet station. "Follow me!" follows that. I stare at the buck knife as if it is no different than a compass, because for me it isn't. What am I supposed to do with this? Cut open a baked potato?

Of course, the zombies are like frat boys pouring towards Dave Matthews by now, coming from everywhere, done with the rodents, the mice and rats and even cats and raccoons and possum and stray dogs, mere appetizers only satiating so much of the hunger.

I debate doing the first peel out of my driving career right about now, leaving Ivan to either be their salad for a zombie or the one of 'em he's destined to become, whichever comes first. Somehow, however, I have the wherewithal to not only realize the wrongness of that, but also the stupidity. After all, he ain't that far gone. He's my ticket to the airwaves, and possibly outta this mess.

In short, Ivan is all I've got. Sure, even though he seems fine right now, and turning zombie could be like Alzheimer's for all I know: A slight detour here and there and then one day finding your way home is straight up impossible. But, the now is just that...THE NOW.

Thus, I do as I am told. I pop the trunk and roll towards the back of the station behind him. Soon enough Ivan is in pure assembly line mode, taking down zombies and tossing ammo into the trunk, an assembly line rhythm heretofore unseen.

Then, he is in the car, telling me to step on it, New York cabbie and all that. Maybe New York is where we will head, I think, across state lines, past the blockades, lone survivors. But they wouldn't let us, would they? I've seen enough movies to know that.

Still, I speed away. I only glance in the rearview mirror once and when I do I see them all chasing after us. Well, chasing isn't exactly the best word—but they are definitely endeavoring to follow us. One falls—a female—by some shrubbery. It looks as if she is then dragged into the bushes, most likely by others who have deemed pursuing us futile. Then again, they couldn't possibly be capable of that thought process. Even so, it definitely looks as if she is being dragged backwards, but my adrenaline is pumping at a rate never before reached, and Ivan may've peed himself a bit more, so I can't be sure.

"Try the radio," he says, huffing, puffing, and looking decidedly pasty. One vein in the side of his face is a shade of blue I've never seen, protruding and map-like.

There is nothing but static. Ivan begins punching the buttons himself, as if it's a high school locker combination. But, lo and behold, he does find a faint signal.

"Long Island," he says, more to himself than to me.

"The beats keep comin'," a deejay announces, which manages to make me cringe, the baritone and bravado as passé as fondue and Tab. "Black-Eyed Peas, Usher, Beyonce and more headin' your way, plus your tickets to the Remember Connecticut Jam..."

Then he's into a stop-set and I can only repeat what he's just said, wanting to be sure I heard right, more to myself than to Ivan: "Did he say Remember Connecticut?"

"Green Day has just been added to the bill," deejay-by-way-of-Rick-Dees adds. Salt, meet wound. I likened Green Day's *American Idiot* record to *Abbey Road* and was eviscerated in the local newspaper. "Zero Credibility at this point" my review was deemed. This stung, as I am a diehard Beatles fan and it was a big enough thing even to say it, to compare anyone modern day to them; what I had meant was Billie Joe and the gang had nailed the concept record, and it was reminiscent of *Abbey Road* in its wingspan (McCartney pun intended), from up-tempo to piano-driven and then back again. But, I never *used* the word "reminiscent," unfortunately. I mean, who would on adult contemporary radio? Bad enough a Green Day song had found its way there, but they actually had years before. In any event, in retort I unleashed a diatribe about the local media. More anger. Thus, more anger management. I may have even called the columnist an "effeminate hack with nothing but hand-me-down Kool & the Gang 45's that constitute his credibility." Something like that.

Anyway. Ivan does not confirm my "Remember Connecticut" inquiry. He does not look well, and why would he? He may even be, at this exact moment, picking a chunk of the right side of his face off. He definitely appears to be tearing at something.

"I say we head straight for New York," I tell him, despite his self-examination. "Obviously."

"The only thing that's obvious there is that the

43

military will either shoot us dead when we hit the state line or whisk us away to some facility full of mental patients and Nurse Ratchets."

"Why would they shoot us dead? Don't you think that story would...oh, I dunno...leak?"

"This many years in the industry," Ivan says with an air of superiority, " and you still haven't learned that some stories just don't leak. Ever."

"Okay, where to then?" I ask, frustrated yet suspecting that Ivan is probably correct. "My station? Get on the air and corral who ever is left in this state? One old adage still applies, Ivan. There's strength in numbers."

"True. And the *zombies outnumber us*," he says. It sounds as if his finger is actually inside his right cheek, fishing for cartilage. "But you want on the air and I'll get you on the air. If it's the last thing I do. Which it probably will be."

"So..." I dangle, fishing myself, albeit figuratively, awaiting a bite. Finally: "The radio station then? My radio station?"

Ivan turns to face me, and I have to take a look, even though I am driving streets rampant with the undead, fraught with the frightful. What he's been pawing at is either an ingrown hair or there's something *inside* his cheek. "Nope," he says, unfazed. "The state police barracks."

Chapter 6:
The End of the World
As We Know It

I am beginning to question Ivan's reliability. Him telling me to head to the state police barracks is both perplexing and pointless. I know, I probably should have begun questioning his reliability the moment I saw the claw-marks or bite-marks or whatever zombie calling card has been left on his arm and, in fact, I did.

Still, I assumed the slow, lingering descent into zombiedom would be just that: slow and lingering. As such, I had made the decision to utilize his engineering skills until he was no longer necessary and then...well...do away with him. I don't know how, but that was the plan.

This state police barracks road trip, though...is it to load up on more weapons and ammunition? Two guys can only carry so many guns. Besides, if the entire undead population arose from their tombs, I gotta figure there ain't enough ammo, or forearm manageability, to take care of that anyway.

Is it an effort to enlist more human aid, and *adept at survival* human aid? I guess that could make sense, if Ivan hadn't reiterated constantly and with such conviction that he didn't think there were any humans left, outside of us.

So why go there?

"Even though radio has gone the Goddamn way of every single thing pre-taped, not a minute spontaneous, DJ Zom-B is gonna have ta do the same," he says, as if he is reading my mind. "We're gonna record you and then rebroadcast it across the state. Even cop the crawl across the TV screens."

"And you think there're folks out there watching TV right now?"

"Fuck, no," Ivan snaps back. "I don't even think there's anybody else alive. Not in Connecticut anyway. But you don't seem to care about that."

As he is saying the words "about that," I, for the first time since the madness, begin wondering why my thought process is actually what it is. Why am I so sure there are others alive? Is it instinctual? My instincts haven't necessarily served me well in my life, neither personally nor professionally. What am I hoping to accomplish by going on the air? Maybe I merely *want* to confirm there either are or aren't other survivors, but even if there are, why would they be watching TV or listening to the radio? One mention of the Remember Connecticut charity concert and in the towel would go—they'd serve themselves up to zombies, intentionally or unintentionally. One way or another they'd wind up not unlike those girls who act as plates to sushi for the rich and shameless. Just, without the plates.

That's it. I need to believe there are others roaming the streets of the Nutmeg State, curled up in its corners, fetal and futile, awaiting a hero...a voice in the darkness. Shit, maybe Ivan is right. Maybe this is all about ego. I say as much. "Maybe this *is* all about ego, Ivan."

"Ya think?" he shoots back heartily. "Whatever. It means more weapons for me, and a couple dozen more zombies who are gonna fall at my hands."

He looks alarmingly excited by this. I don't wanna ruin it for him by mentioning the probability of zombie police.

I pillage my mind for more zombie lore. The thought of zombie police triggers this "memory bank heist."

Yes, there could be zombies who were law enforcement less than 24 hours earlier when we reach the barracks; shit, if there are, their tattered uniforms will alert us to that very fact. But, even so, they would not have the skill set or acumen to work firearms. The zombies are exactly what Romero led us all to believe from what I'm seeing: They are mindless, groaning entities hell-bent on one thing and one thing only, and that's feeding. Then again, it's not even feeding as much as it is simply destroying anything living, really. They stroll by abandoned automobiles and feel no urge to smash in a windshield, by a parking meter and do not endeavor to bend it backwards, by a stop sign and do not pluck it like a flower, by a...well, you get the picture.

Further, running one over with a mail truck cannot kill it, and so I ruminate: decapitation is truly the way to go. Beyond that a shotgun blast through the chest cavity. Suffocation is not a viable option.

There is not a Frankenstein variation, meaning while they appear keen on groaning and moaning, they cannot utter a single, solitary word. Indeed my contact thus far has been limited, but I did walk among them and heard nada. And running from them did not generate even one "Stop!"

* * * * *

We are on the highway. Don't even recall the on-ramp. Ivan is pointing, and it's visibly hurting him to do so. I don't know if it is because of constant firearm usage, physical altercation, his age, a culmination of all, or the fact that said arm could fall off at any moment. I don't ask. I don't want to know. We are on "need to know" status indefinitely.

"There!" he shouts, as if I missed him saying it already, although, to be fair, I did not respond to the pointing verbally or even via nodding. The state police barracks are straight ahead, nestled behind a Mobil gas station. The building looks remarkably untouched, unscathed—not so much as a window broken. A squad car sits out front, pristine almost, a sheen from the reemerging sun cascading off a recent wax job and causing a glare, yet not any hope whatsoever.

The whole scene is suspect in its lack of chaos, a signpost if ever there was one, in my opinion. I mention this.

"The place looks perfect. Too perfect. That seems weird to me." Ivan says nothing in reply.

I pull alongside the parked squad car, slowly, ready to floor it at the slightest sound, even if that sound was a squirrel polishing off some Dunkin' Donuts on an empty front seat. Ivan gets out, car still moving notwithstanding. He cocks one of his weapons and blasts the front door open.

Which may have been unlocked.

Which was the type of entrance I didn't want to make.

You tiptoe around zombies, do you not?

Never mind the waste of ammo.

Ivan's movie life was clearly a steady diet of *Apocalypse Now*, *Full Metal Jacket*, and *Platoon*.

Nonetheless, I throw the car into park, hop out, and follow him in, practically hugging his estimable shadow. Far as I'm concerned he just hollered, "Come and get it!"

"Why would you announce us like that?" I ask through gritted teeth.

"Because they should fear me," he says calmly, confidently. "Us, I mean."

"But...they don't have fear," I remind him. "These zombies...*can't*...fear."

"Well," Ivan begins, pausing only to kick in a door with a colorful logo on it that is several circles within one large circle and a lightning bolt jutting into that, thus begging the question of why he didn't just kick the other door open, "class is in session."

It's official. Nick Nolte will be playing him in the movie.

We approach another door and Ivan pauses to read a laminated sheet of paper thumb-tacked to it that boasts the headline, "Activation Procedures." I, in turn, take the time to survey our surroundings. Again, oddly (to me, that is), the place seems untouched. All of the weapons remain, from handguns to rifles, the latter staring defiantly at me from a glass case hung on the wall, no different than a B.B. King or Clapton autographed guitar at a Hard Rock Café. This strikes me as bizarre. If no one took the weapons that means they themselves may have been taken by surprise. Yet there's no sign of struggle, of a disturbance of any kind, not so much as a paper out of place, never mind a drop of blood on the floor. Or anywhere else for that matter. It's as if they all just punched out like any other day.

Speaking of papers being out of place—or, rather, not being out of place—I pick one up off a random desk. It is a Google list of cemeteries in the vicinity.

Suddenly a pair of pants hits me in the head, with a velocity that throttles me a bit.

"What the fuck!?" I counter, looking at Ivan angrily.

"Put 'em on and stop playing detective. There ain't nothin' to solve here," he commands.

"Says you."

"Really? A radio host for how many years, and a 'says you.' What's next, sticks and stones..."

I look down at the pants. They're the bottom half of a police uniform. While I realize impersonating an officer isn't going to get me in any legal hot water at the moment, it's also a complete waste of time.

"Think zombies fear the fuzz, do we?"

"No," Ivan says without looking up, still digesting the activation procedures. "Think you smell like piss."

Poor bastard doesn't even know the stink is coming from him.

* * * * *

"Um...hello. Hello. This is...um...Luke Zombulli. Um..."

That's three um's. Every radio host counts his or her um's or, at the very least, is acutely, painfully aware of them. Said awareness usually results in a few more.

"I don't know who is hearing this. If anyone is hearing this, really. Um...I don't even know what to say to anyone who...well...um...*is* hearing this."

Two more. I am crouched over a transmitter and talking into a microphone no different than the kind my friends and I used to use to record our acapella renditions of Guns 'n Roses into our tape recorders with. Ivan is clearly amused by my regression as a broadcaster.

"Maybe that it's okay? That you're not alone?" I continue despite his amusement. My heart rate accelerates, the rhythm that can actually come from fumbling rising up through my chest, causing it to heave. It's like when you're representing the radio station at a dance party and no one in the club wants to hear you try to be cool or even likes the station you're working for, alternately tossing hateful bon mots, stringy lemon wedges, and sloppy ice cubes. But you recover and get their attention, turn it around. Probably because of that.

My voice raises, gets confident. "Listen, if you can hear me now, I am at the state police barracks. I have weapons and a vehicle. I am not alone." I glance over at Ivan. "For long."

Ivan and I don't look at one another as I place the microphone down. He presses some buttons, that diabolical way that engineers or producers do.

"Gotta find the pattern," he says aloud.

"Pattern?"

51

"Code," he clarifies. Although it really doesn't.

The numbers flashing are red, and he punch, punch, punches away...

Then, green. Green is always go. Green is good. The earth used to be green. Well, most of it still is, just not Connecticut, Nevada, and one other place in between. Or Maine.

"Goddamn," Ivan purrs. "It's retransmitting!" He shouts it like one would have "gold" in the old days or even "eureka." He hoists himself up and raises his hand for a high-five. I oblige. His shirt bunches up as we do so and that zombie scratch or bite rears its ugly head again. I can't help but to look at it. It's more a gash than anything, with blue spider webs reaching out from it in every direction, infection nibbling away.

He notices me noticing it and locks eyes on me. Not in a good way either. But then the strangest thing happens.

The phone rings.

Chapter 7:
Call Waiting

Ivan stares at the phone as it continues to ring. I get the feeling he truly thinks zombies are capable of dialing a phone, maybe the quintessential crank call... "Is your refrigerator running? Well, chase after it!" Bunch o' zombies laughing in the background. It is as if all of his encounters with the undead thus far have not educated him in the least bit.

Or maybe I'm just reading him wrong. God knows that's a strong suit. Even if God doesn't seem all that plausible an entity at this particular time.

I wedge myself loose from his grip, walk over and answer. The phone is ancient, a rotary phone and heavy as a cinder block. The receiver feels like close to the weight I used to curl with when I thought there was more time.

"H-hello?" I say, sheepishly, a 180 from the radio-phone-answering me. Answering the phone with zeal is a must for the morning radio host, which I had even begun doing at home, friends always jokingly asking if they were the correct caller or inquiring what they won when calling me.

"Is...um...is this Luke?" I hear. A man. A quivering mess of a man.

"Yes," I confirm. "Yes it is."

"Is this a...a...trap?" He sounds terrified. Old, too. Or at least, older.

"Zombies don't have the intellect to set traps, sir."

"I wasn't thinking zombies," he says, which makes absolutely no sense. But before I can ask him to clarify...

"We have a bus. We can get to you," he says. "Strength in numbers."

I want to ask what kind of bus. I want to ask who "we" is, and if it includes anyone who might really be able to fight, to even lead, get bios and such, but the questions just swim in my head. I'm too busy beginning to wonder about Ivan's descent, and what my real "plan" actually is.

"Yes! Yes, strength in numbers," I say back firmly.

"People I'm with know you," he tells me. This makes sense, of course, having been an on-air personality in Connecticut for so many years, so I don't think to probe. Not outside asking "How many are with you," that is.

"Five," he replies dramatically. I don't know if that's the right word. He basically says it in a way that suggests that an hour or so ago the answer was different.

"Counting you?" I persist.

"Six counting me," he corrects. "How 'bout with you?"

"Two," I tell him. I want add something along the lines of "for now," but what good would that do? And would they even come if they knew Ivan's zombie alarm clock had been set, no snooze option? Doubtful.

"Two with you?"

"Two including me." It's an obscenely morose variation of *Who's On First?* I then ask, "How did you hear me anyway?" But before he can tell me Ivan plucks the phone from my shaky grip.

"Can you teenagers skip the Chatty Kathy bullshit?" Then, into the phone: "Just get here." He slams the phone down. We look at each other intensely again, but this time it's different. It's like he just did that for me. His eyes appear soulful. Ivan wants to save me. From him, I think.

The first concert I ever went to was Ozzy Osbourne. I was fourteen. I remember it pretty vividly mostly because of the guy who introduced the show. He was a local radio personality, a real big shot at the rock station in town. This was the day and age when a deejay could still make a hit record happen, go against the grain and play any random track he chose on an album—yes, album—and say something like, "This isn't the single but it should be."

And then people would call.

And then it WOULD be the single.

Doing that very same thing, in the gilded Seacrest age, has become grounds for dismissal. Payola equals crap-ola, we all know that; shit, that goes back to the 1950's. But, the deejay still had an elbowroom of sorts, up until 2000 or so. Then rigidity and inflexibility became the norm, and reporting every slight deviation from the play-list became mandatory, every talk break clocking in at no more than three minutes. Stifling, creativity a flame easily smothered.

This was the 1980's, though, either the Bark at the Moon *tour or maybe* Tribute, *the cross-country homage to*

Randy fucking Rhodes. This radio host took the stage like he was lending it to Ozzy for the night. The cheers for him rivaled those the bat-eating rocker got himself, never mind the God-awful opening act. He commanded the stoned attendees shout the call letters of the station back at him, and they did, a different way every time; one time all together fast, one time the first letter dragged out ad nauseum ("doublllllleeeeee-youuuuuuuuu!!!!!) and the next three strung together, one time all four letters standing along, strong, indivisible.

For the remainder of the night everyone just did the same thing, on repeat, a record skipping: pumping their fists, in unison, in a trance, entranced. I walked among the concertgoers, straying from my Schnapps-swilling chaperones, from the last row on the floor up to the twentieth, then the fifteenth, then the tenth...

They all looked the same, wore the same blank expressions, and the fists pumped and pumped and pumped, robotically, beat be damned. During Goodbye to Romance *they swapped the fist-pumping for lighter-waving, yet still the choreography remained in tact, and it was like the entire crowd, the whole long since defunct New Haven Coliseum audience had rehearsed together, like they all were given a "how-to" guide.*

Bottles were being thrown from the upper sections, smashing around those on the floor, missing heads by inches, but still they pumped their fists, shouted "Ozzy, Ozzy, Ozzy!"

Around the fifth row I was asked to show my ticket. I did. Security escorted me up and out, onto the cold Elm City street where I had to wait out two encores. My ride came out and I strode up alongside him, but he didn't even acknowledge me, hadn't even noticed I was gone, or so it seemed.

And the rest of the sold-out crowd flooded onto the street, fists still pumping, like the music hadn't even stopped.

Chapter 8:
Bussed In

"Wake up, Zombie-town. You do not have to hide in the shadows, crossing your fingers, wondering if the undead can actually hear hearts beating or smell human flesh...like I did for more days than I care to remember. They can, but whatever. We are gathering forces. We have taken over the state police barracks on the parkway and are assembling an army of our own. Connecticut is not a place to be remembered. We don't have to be one collective possum playing dead."

Ivan nods. He likes that last part.

"Nobody is coming in after us, looking to save our sorry asses...at least, not so far, anyway. And they may not let us leave, for fear of contamination. I cannot claim to know what the government is thinking. Never have, never will. All I've ever been is a guy with a microphone. But, if you can hear me, there's hope."

"Tell 'em your name," urges Ivan.

"My name is Luke, and I'm..."

"Nah, tell 'em your radio name."

I cover the microphone. "Don't you think calling myself DJ Zom-B is a tad—I dunno—insensitive considering our circumstances?"

Ivan tilts his head like a curious mongrel. "People *know* DJ Zom-B. Nobody knows Luke."

I take my hand off the microphone and finish. "...also known as DJ Zom-B. Ironic, right? But maybe even...fitting."

Click.

Pound.

Enter. The system and the ether.

Ivan and I listen for the phone but this time it doesn't ring. What we do hear, however, is the sound of a vehicle approaching. I pull a curtain to the side and peer out the unwashed window; I can make out the front end of the bus, and its left tire is dangerously low, if not flat. It's like a limping beast, moving slowly but surely in our direction.

As it emerges from the steam coming off the ground, light rain being fried by sudden burst of sun, I can see that it is not a city bus. It's also not a school bus.

What it is, is a tour bus. And across the side of it, in all its graffiti-esque glory, is *Mercedes*.

"Oh, great," I can hear myself say in a whisper, mostly to myself.

"No shit," Ivan says, same way. Then he turns to me and adds, "A handful of cockroaches left in Connecticut and one's a pop star. A fuckin' pop star survived!"

He's full-on laughing now, out the door and on his way to greet our guests. The first person out of the bus is an older man of I'd say sixty or so, with a woman about the same age right behind him. I'm lousy with matching ages to folks, but that's what I'd guess. His paunch and her hips are twins.

"Pop star and the geriatrics!" Ivan shouts by way of greeting. It's as if he's deemed them a new singing group. The Mamas and the Papas redux.

"I'm Stan," the gentleman says, extending his hand. Ivan clumsily turns his attention from the gesture, keenly aware that the moment anyone spots his wound he'll probably be bound and gagged, at best. "Um, I'm the one you spoke to on the phone," Stan adds, noticing.

"To me," I intervene. "You spoke to me." I walk over and take his hand into mine, or more the other way around; his is the size of a sledgehammer, a lifetime of loading docks and chopping lumber, judging from the grip and amount of calluses. It's like the mitt is covered in Crazy Glue, his skin under a protective layer of scale. His shoulders are so high and broad it makes it appear as if he is presently in a stockade.

"You're the deejay then. Good to meet you. This my wife, Mary-Beth." I take her hand into mine, and this time it's the truth; hers is trembling, bones like straw. "Our hostess knows you."

That's when Mercedes steps out, flanked by her boy-toy Smack and a suit-and-tie total record exec guy. Her label guy hits a stride like he owns the street, even while he is clearly having Blackberry withdrawal, clocking in at a whopping 5'2", the poster boy for Napoleon complex.

As for Smack, he is the same as I always remembered him, ever the zero body fat metrosexual brains of the operation. His $300 skintight jeans cannot be serving him well at this particular time, nor his clingy Diesel tee. Furthermore, neither does his five o'clock shadow, grooming gone the way of safety, his notorious goatee now obsolete, or, moreover, billygoat-ish. Why I'm noticing all this is beyond me, given the present situation.

"Zom-B," Smack says. "Of all the sellouts to survive. Pains me to say that name. For a whole variety of reasons. Obviously."

Oh, right. That's why I'm noticing all this. Smack and I hate each other. He wanted to *give* me a smack when I did one particular skit about Mercedes on my show (there have been Lindsay Lohan many), no doubt your standard-issue unreciprocated producer crush the catalyst.

"Hello, Mercedes," I say, completely ignoring Smack. She looks frazzled, not the confident pop star I know and shove.

In other words, obviously her makeup artist hasn't made it.

But, then again, Mercedes' downward spiral no doubt included the cutting loose of said makeup artist, along with other assorted hangers on and "yes" folks. Still, downtrodden or no, terrified or no, there is something alluring about the girl; I never thought she was necessarily weighed down by talent, anchored to studio floors by artistic necessity, but she does have a certain quality. And it's not just that she's hot; there's a soul there. She'd probably sell it right about now to keep her living thing going, but still. Then again, saying a pop star would sell his or her soul ain't saying much, now is it?

"Hey," is all she can manage to say back, sans eye contact. Smack looks on, as if mentally jotting the whole thing down, wanting to record for all eternity just how much interest in my existence his golden girl may or may not show and/or showed. Zilch. For the record.

It is difficult in such a precarious situation not to revisit the whole "last man on earth" scenario, one uttered to so many a fool-hearted man during less turbulent days, and often thought to himself; this truly was that time, facetiousness aside.

Last man in Connecticut anyway.

And Nevada.

And that one other place.

And probably Maine by now, too.

That said, the competition isn't all that steep, and Mercedes is the crème de la crème. You can count the old guy's wife but that'd be like counting Mrs. Howell on *Gilligan's Island*. Sure, we only had Ginger—not a Mary-Ann in sight, but I like to think there's a Mary-Ann beneath each Ginger I've ever met.

Suddenly, all of the women in my life flickered like a slide show in my mind's eye and I regretted losing or letting go not a single solitary one since the first broke my high school heart. Three weeks and a prom was all it took for that heartbreak. We didn't even have sex. While I did with all of those who followed, none so much as resonated a third as much as she. The sadness of this reality was a mallet to my memory bank.

As it shattered, the hum of yet another engine is heard in the distance, ever closer, perhaps much like our collective demise.

But, then I rethink that pessimism. My latest broadcast must've reached others! We all turn in unison, and see a tried-n-true paddy wagon heading towards us. Ivan lunges for his weapon, still frighteningly certain zombies can drive. They could surely work at the DMV, but not drive.

"Uh oh," says record label guy.

"Is that an armored car?" Stan wonders aloud. I'd never noticed before that the armored car and a paddy wagon are both so structurally similar, one toting bundles of cash and/or brick upon brick of gold, and the other full of those who would steal those very contents, leaving dead bodies behind if need be, alibis well-rehearsed but typically as weak as the public defender's case.

"Paddy wagon," Ivan tells him, but he is loath to drop his weapon.

"Ivan," I urge him, "take it down a notch." My gesture to lower it is dismissed. "Dude, they'll blast you. They're police who've been in survival mode for almost an entire week."

"They're also police who might just want to blast *us*."

"I'm with Buford," chimes in record label guy.

"Blast us?" Mary-Beth repeats. "Why would the police want to...to...blast us?" She is a quivering mess, and Stan wraps his arm around her tightly. "They're the police, for heaven's sake."

"Of course they are," record label guy interjects with an air of superiority that manages to exist sans the death of all his toys. "Oh, dear, they could never be crooked!"

"Sir, don't mock my wife," Stan says, the "sir" coming from such an obvious gentleman to such an obvious ass, never mind from someone more than twice his age succeeding in riling me. It's been a lifetime of being riled, of various medications and exercises to quell the riling. "I know where you stand on the police. I know you say you saw one engage one of these creatures and don't understand why he didn't just kill it. But that doesn't mean you can disrespect my wife."

"What's your name anyway?" I ask.

"Alex," comes the answer, delivered as if he'd prefer to be delivering a baby or, moreover, the news that his latest discovery just went Gold. "Van Olsen. Crunch Records."

"Crunch. Hah!" scoffs Ivan. "A branch on Sony's tree that shoulda been pruned two years ago."

Ivan's seeming grasp on the intricacies of an industry Alex felt solely privy to, Mercedes and Smack included, clearly throws Alex momentarily, his tiny hand tearing through his decidedly non-tiny mane of hair—and I mean "little person" tiny! Then he clumsily endeavors to tuck a $500 shirt back into its twice-as-costly pants, his hope to appear impeccable amongst such chaos laughable—if anyone were capable of laughing, that is.

"I remember you from Crunchapolooza," Ivan adds. "Head engineer."

Increasingly awkward, unflinchingly arrogant, Alex fires back, "That explains a lot."

"Not about the lack of attendance," continues Ivan, not the slightest bit bored of antagonizing the label lackey. But does the lackey know the label still exists? That his Blackberry is shut down because they're presuming him dead, and moving on accordingly? If Alex and Co. heard me then they heard about the "Remember Connecticut" concert, right? They *had* to.

But before the heated exchange could escalate any farther, the paddy wagon doors fly open, the beast's wings immense, creaking and foreboding. Two figures piled out.

First up, the driver, a burly, hirsute, heavily inked—and much of it homemade—bonafide officer of the law. He is calm, cool, and collect*ing*—people, that is, judging from the pounding taking place inside the wagon. His jaw is a mass of bone, jutting out and concrete, the roots of his teeth clearly twice the necessary size and resistant to any removal, particularly by fist, or butt of a handgun. He laughs in Ivan's direction.

"You can lower your weapon, Larry the Cable Guy. Case you haven't noticed, I'm the law."

"The law could be overhead right about now, too, in helicopters, plucking our sorry asses from this dead state. But, they ain't," replies Ivan stoically.

"And that has to do *what* with us exactly? With why you're aiming a gun at me? Which is getting on my nerves, by the way."

"You know what's getting on *my* nerves?" Alex interjects frantically. "The pounding in your fucking cruiser here. They're crooks, for chrissakes! Where are they gonna go? If they run, it's fucking feeding time!"

With that Alex bolts for the rear of the vehicle, and uses both his mini-hands to undo the latch.

"Don't do that!!!" screams the "law."

But, it's too late. A zombie lurches forward and begins feeding on Alex's face, a horrific variation on bobbing for apples. Its hands are tied behind its back. The assault is vicious, bloody, and unrelenting.

"Zombie!" shrieks Mercedes.

"Yeah? What!?" answers Zom-B. Me.

"No! *Zombie*!!" Mercedes shrieks it differently now, and points.

The undead man spats Alex's nose out onto the street and it bounces towards my feet. Mary-Beth pukes on the back of her husband Stan's head.

"*Fuck*," the law harrumphs, and then ups and tasers

the zombie into submission, and then slams the door back on, presumably, several more of the undead, taking the foot of one clear off. There is a foot, a nose, and more on the ground. It looks like Mr. Potato head exploded.

Alex just drops to his knees, a hole where his face was. The law's deputy empties a round into him after the law gives him the high sign to do just that.

"Jesus..." is all Smack can muster up the wherewithal to say. Deputy drags the body over to the grass.

"Jesus he definitely *wasn't*," Mercedes adds, simultaneously kissing the crucifix on her necklace.

Click.

Ivan's gun is presently pressed against the back of the deputy's head, the cocking of it alerting the law to this latest turn of events.

"And why exactly..." Ivan begins, "are we blowing holes through the humans and not the doornails?"

There's a staring contest. Ivan wins. Hands down.

"Fucker had no face. Not like he was gonna live. We put him outta his misery. Now, could you lower that? I am the law, after all. Officer Letchcow. Thirty years on the force."

"Still waitin' on the why-we're-keeping-zombies-alive explanation," Ivan tells him, unflinching. As always.

"But," Letchcow says coolly, "they aren't alive to begin with."

"Semantics, Letch. Yer deputy here won't be in a sec, either, you keep this crap up."

"That's good, that's good," Letchcow admits, smirking. "And folks do call me Letch. Have since grade school."

"Your reputation precedes you," Ivan informs him.

"Another reason I'm still holdin' this baby up."

Letch appears a mixture of amused and agitated. Clearly he's made some headlines over the years—the kind Top 40 radio hosts miss but the talk radio guys chew up, spit out, and ride into syndication, enemies made and stepped over all at the same time. His smile—if you can call it one—reveals one monster tooth, but it's nipping at his bottom lip, looking like he's causing himself a little bit of pain to keep him from going off. He likes being known but not right now, not right here.

"It's us against them, Cable Guy. Why off 'em for a second time when figurin' them out might just help us in the long run?"

Sounds good to me. To all of us, in fact, judging from the collective exhale. Ivan lowers his weapon.

"Christ," says the deputy. "Take long enough? I'm Nate." He extends his hand to Ivan. "Pleased to meet you. I appreciate your paranoia. 'Specially at a time like this. We sure are being contained, and that's the right thing. Once the unscathed survivors are assessed by the proper authorities we'll be allowed to cross state lines safely."

"Assessed?" Ivan repeats. "Nate?" Says that the same way. Both things irk him, the use of the word "assess" and the deputy's name.

"Put a lid on the pep talk, deputy," commands Letch. "And transport our captives. Holding cells according to gender."

"They're zombies, dude," Smack points out. I notice he's holding Mercedes' wrist, not her hand. While distracted, she seems oddly at ease. I mean, her label guy's face was just eaten off in front of her—someone she's worked with for years, side by side, radio station to radio station, live performances on morning shows with "zany" hosts at six in the morning, private concerts for contest winners at chain restaurants in the banquet room. They probably even fucked.

Maybe she's in shock?

"'Dude'? Really? That strikes you as smart?" Letch responds. "How 'bout we all just get inside, hole these monstrosities up, get cleaned up, and maybe see if we can choke down some food ourselves?"

Mary-Beth likes that. She giggles nervously at the mere mention of food. She also just emptied her belly out onto her husband, so why wouldn't she?

* * * * *

Mercedes was the *Next Big Thing*. Are there three more daunting words, other than *I Love You*?

She did a slew of shows whose title was exactly that, *Next Big Thing*, or it was in there somewhere, proof of the demise of original thought if ever there was any; one network, one cable, one internet, one acronymed ("N.B.T.," hosted by a male Asian-American who went only by Wang, and without a trace of facetiousness), plus she did a spread in many a magazine wherein *Next Big Thing* was the headline. *Next Big Thing* is a rake many a recording artist steps on. Or is shoved onto is more like it.

Mercedes' next record—the words "sophomore slump" bandied about before the first track was even recorded—saw her bring a fresh-from-rehab drummer and songwriter with punk rock cred to write and produce, and also her penning half of the disc's tracks herself. Two kisses of death. One for each cheek, if you will.

During recording she let cameras follow her around as she dated the co-star of a CW drama called *Drama Queen*, the secondary character's best guy friend, a nice enough fella named Chad Bawling. This was for a reality TV show that never materialized—meaning never got picked up—myriad potential titles smudged on paper filling Viacom wastebaskets. Rumors swirled that the CW, with *Drama Queen* entering its third season, was who squashed it, and even more that Mercedes' label was the culprits; she found the latter laughable, as she felt like Crunch forgot she so much as existed after her first world tour generated mediocre reviews and revenue. Smack assured her this wasn't the case, but his intense gaze—hearts practically forming over his head like out of an Archie comic book—suggested his pep talks, as they were, were generated by something decidedly different than artistic temperament.

Mercedes owned the second stage of a *Lilith Fair* knock-off, performance-wise. While the "names" procured the big crowds it was Mercedes who truly delivered, smack dab next to jerk chicken kiosks and tie-dyed tee-shirt purveyors, bopping to prerecorded beats yet hammering home messages about individuality, female empowerment, following your heart, et al. It would not later be discovered that she was the result of a privileged Manhattan upbringing, a private school product of unparalleled pedigree, adept at navigating the streets of SoHo from the back of a limo; no, she was Mercedes from the Block, a public school expatriate whose negligent father forced her into catharsis after catharsis, first with the paint brush and later with the microphone. After all, you can hold both the same way.

Smack looked on at everything, heart just under his sleeve, but if she cared to look close enough Mercedes would clearly see it beating. He was okay with her choice of songwriting partner on the second record, even thought it was a bold, ambitious move; sure, he wanted in on the collaborative process and had even been offered a solo deal but declined—for the time being, acutely aware of the message that would send, an additional one to a litany of negative ones.

What was decidedly more difficult for Smack to watch was Mercedes laughable dalliance with Chad. It was all so contrived, so hatched at a Crunch roundtable; but Chad wasn't just ducking out of the hotel room after the paparazzi vanished, going back to his room or apartment, where a real girlfriend lay in wait. Nope, he was getting all of the perks associated with having a real girlfriend. Smack wrestled with this one as a man in love but even more so as someone who was losing respect for an artist.

Still, he stood by her, a captain going down with his ship, the proximity to her being payoff enough. The second record dropped, and then really dropped.

Smack and Mercedes used to walk the Crunch halls together, bottled water being thrust toward them, offers of anything under the sun, CD's flipped open and autographs begged for; a week after the release of *Love U 2 Pieces*—a superior song to her "hit" in every way, by the way—they walked the halls receiving nary a glance, tense, lumbering suits feigning important calls. They looked as if they might be speaking to her but it was all Bluetooth. They just came at Smack and Mercedes, stiff and mumbling. Like zombies.

71

Chapter 9:
Caged

Settled—inasmuch as we all could be given the circumstances—into the office area, everyone is noshing on the contents of the vending machine. Those of us who *can* eat, that is.

The feast is a veritable stoner's delight: Doritos, salt & vinegar potato chips, pretzels, Skittles, Starburst, peanut M&M's and more. Standard vending machine fare.

"Caught yer broadcast," Letch finally says, puncturing the balloon of silence (excluding Stan's impressive crunching). "Clever."

"Thank him," I say, deferring to Ivan.

"You mean *blame* him," Nate offers. "If that aired nationwide we'd get a bomb dropped on us. Connecticut would be a memory."

"It already is," Ivan replies. "Shit. They're having a 'Remember Connecticut' concert, for Chrissakes."

"What my deputy is saying, in case you misunderstood, is that if you see any helicopters overhead don't go waving your arms. Find a bush and jump on in."

"Whoa, whoa, hold up a sec," Smack interjects, simultaneously smacking on Skittles. Figures. Such a girl's candy. "'Remember Connecticut?' Concert? Who the hell's playing?" He looks over at Mercedes, who remains nonplused. It simply has to be shock. "Cedes! Did you hear that?"

All she manages to say back is, "Alex is dead."

"Can we boot up in here?" Ivan asks.

"You wanna shoot dope? In a state police barracks? Undead uprising or no..."

"Pipe down, deputy," Letch interrupts, laughingly, waving his hand. "He means the computer. United Fates site, am I right?"

Ivan is displeased that he and this man could be on the same page, communicating without even really saying anything to one another.

"You showin' these pop tarts that stupid site will not only succeed in freaking them out even more, but it'll drain the generator. Not enough juice and we gotta get through the night."

"Right, and we need the lights on for the somnambulists. They gotta be able to find us, after all."

Ivan and Letch have a Quinn/Sheriff Brody thing happening, except for two things: They might not be looking to accomplish the same task, and there was only *Jaws*—one Great White shark in Long Island water; this is a river of blood that hundreds of zombies are swimming in.

"Som what?" Stan inquires, the amount of chips in his mouth muffling his speech slightly.

"Somnambulist," Letch tells him. "Fancy word for

zombie or ghoul. Ivan here just has somethin' to prove with me. Impressive, though. Gotta admit. Prefer your 'doornails,' though."

The incarcerated zombies are remarkably quiet. The constant hum of their groaning seemed like it would rise up from the few holding cells in the basement of the barracks. I begin to wonder if Letch simply instructed his deputy to lop each of their heads off, and this was all one gigantic mind-fuck he was orchestrating. There were only a handful, though; maybe they pipe down when no humans are around...

"Can I go to sleep?" Mercedes asks, apropos of nothing. Why she thinks she needs someone's permission for this is beyond me, even if Letch has somehow commandeered our little group. A badge and air of superiority can have that effect, I suppose.

I cannot help but wonder how she would even be able to sleep. That's when all of my wondering about Mercedes crashes together in a potential heap of understanding: Self-medication. The recording artist's Duracell. As if reading my mind, she snaps the cap to a can of soda, tosses a capsule into her mouth, past her full, succulent lips, and chases it with Sierra Mist. I swear that soft drink is named after a stripper.

"Take the nurse's office down the hall on the right, honey. It's basically the honeymoon suite of the joint. You two can join them in there," Letch says, aiming his stone jaw at Stan and Mary-Beth.

Them? I think to myself, and just as I do Smack stands up, alongside Mercedes, and the foursome—or two couples, I guess you could say—begin to head out the door. "Oh, and one other thing: Nobody goes downstairs.

75

We leave at the break of dawn, too, so get some shut-eye."
Letch props up his feet after that little disclaimer, fatigued
from façade.

"Much as you can sleep with one eye open anyway,"
Nate the deputy adds.

* * * * *

Ivan, my roommate for the evening—you know, the
one who is slowly turning into a zombie and seems to be
the most well-versed, somehow, in their lore—shows no
immediate signs that sleep is on his itinerary. Directly
after deciding on what office we'd be occupying he begins
compulsively tying and untying his bootlaces. Fidgety is
an understatement.

He's peeking through the crack of the door, across the
hall to where Letch and his deputy are, but isn't even
listening intently. Instead he is rambling on about crop
fertilization, delivering a dissertation on the evils of
pesticides to no one in particular—least of all me—and I
am left to assume crop circles will probably be brought up
soon, the surge in the zombie population attributed to
UFOs. I can only then deduce that this is his slow descent
into madness I have a front row seat for, and for the night,
a madness that will ultimately give way to a full on
zombie transformation.

Cool.

It is decided: I cannot go to sleep either. I now begin
mulling over letting Letch in on Ivan's "situation." But
Letch does not necessarily inspire trust. Flipping a coin
crosses my mind. Too bad I don't have one.

I adjourn to the bathroom briefly, perhaps even

subconsciously to assess it for sleeping purposes. I enter just in time to catch Smack washing his shirt in the sink. He doesn't so much as flinch upon my swinging the door open, which amazes me. Zombies have claimed the state, and the cops don't seem all that solid an alternative, and this clown's not the least bit jumpy? Mercedes must be splitting the Valium. An arching of his left eyebrow is all the sudden opening of the door causes.

Smack has muscles in places I didn't think there could be muscles, his sinewy arms are like a toy racecar track, twisting and turning. He begins to squeeze the shirt, to drain it of excess water, and in doing so tendons in his forearms spring forth, not unlike cables one would use to hook up a new television. His waist can't be more than a twenty-six, and mine wasn't that, even at that age. Flipping a coin crosses my mind yet again; Mercedes surely wouldn't have to do that were she forced to choose between Smack and I, for procreation purposes, of course—for the human race to begin anew.

I breeze by him without saying a word, and spot the word "Mercy" tattooed across his upper back, from shoulder to shoulder. Everyone's tattoos either speak of a "mayhem" they are incapable of in the face of it, or a sympathy and/or empathy they will not be shown. After all, zombies are illiterate. In other words, our tattoos mock us in the end. Just, not in that "I'll be the guy on the walker in the old age home with the saggy dragon on my arm" way we all joke upon getting the thing.

At the urinal I glance over at the palm of my right hand as it hovers around the handle, partially upturned and devoid of any signs of hard labor, the polar opposite of Stan's. Outside, of fist-clenching and/or throwing, there is not much wear and tear.

My lifeline is this gigantic parentheses. The open of the parentheses—as opposed to the close—resides there; the close is, interestingly enough, on my left. Have you ever noticed that before? They can only make a parentheses if you cross your arms before yourself, palms aimed inwards.

I've had at least a half dozen palm readers, psychics, and fortune tellers live on the air over the years, yet this is the first time I actually debate the credibility of such a "science." Maybe because I'd rather do it than have an exchange with Smack, a young man who embodies everything that I am not, and both never wanted to be yet would've probably been happier to be. They always said my lifeline was soooo long, these fake eyelash-sporting, tarot card toting shysters, and the past few days do not necessarily contradict that prediction; I also cannot help but to notice how said lifeline sprawls towards my wrist, reaches for it like it's a fucking brass ring, a wave reaching for fleshy shore. I pause to not only acknowledge but—now—celebrate its existence. It's not unlike clinging to a fortune cookie inscription while plummeting from an airplane. Without a chute.

But, am I—nay, are *we*—truly without a chute? I mean, after all, there are armed officers of the law in our company, even if they somehow seem as worthy of our fear as the undead. And there's also the fact that this is apparently not a global turn of events, or even nationwide; this crop-dusting catastrophe is just the latest in a long line of manmade calamity, with a safe haven only miles away. It's just a matter of convincing those protecting that haven that we are still one of them, uncontaminated, a slow descent into flesh-hungry monstrosity not in our foreseeable future. Hey, none of my palm readers ever saw it coming. They didn't see this, either, but still.

"Hell of a coincidence, huh?" Smack's voice rises up like one of his "beats," a familiar, not entirely off-putting monotone.

"That we'd both have to pee?" I reply, pithy as all get out.

"Um...I'm not peeing," he says, his sense of humor not goaded up from the ground along with the dead apparently. "Nor do I use the word peeing."

"Wow. But you use the word 'nor.'"

"Whatever, Has-been. I should be the one being aggressive. You're the asshole who did tired morning radio zoo bits about Mercedes, fucked with her head by putting her in the same category as drug addict Beverly Hills rich girls with reality shows. The coincidence is that you wind up in this hellhole together." Smack's chest twitches just then, pure punctuation, his left nipple not only looking like, but acting as a giant period. Our bodies provide all this punctuation—no wonder we have words written on them.

"Maybe it's fate," I tell him. "Which is really just another word for coincidence."

With that I adjourn, sans washing my hands. I notice Smack notice that, but rather than comment on my hygiene, or lack thereof, he says, "Fate, right. That's what played a big part in that obstacle course radio promotion of yours, wasn't it? Fate dealt that hand."

I don't bite, don't even turn around. As I walk away I hear the distinct sound of a gym rat dropping and launching into a string of push-ups.

I make my way down the hallway and notice that the door down to the bottom floor is cracked open, which it wasn't before. I hear voices. Letch and Nate, eating: big bites and small talk. Impossibly small.

"Guy was on 'Love Boat,' 'Happy Days'..."

"S'what I mean. He always came in at the end."

"Better than that Nancy Boy Marcy was married to."

"No way. Al totally turned that boy around. Got 'em to see the light. Funny shit. Bundy rules."

"Not arguing 'bout Bundy. Talkin' 'bout the neighbor. Jefferson was the man. Didn't they find out he was a spy in the end?"

"Whatever happened to that kid Seven?"

"That was a goddamned Brad Pitt movie, stupid."

They're talking about "Married: With Children!" No, scratch that: They're *arguing* about "Married: With Children;" *debating* it. The "better neighbor debate," which is, admittedly, several steps above the "Better Darren on 'Bewitched'" argument, and maybe one above The Ropers versus Furley, but the insouciance is dumbfounding. They are either completely overconfident in their abilities with regard to capturing, holding and transporting the undead, or completely oblivious to the seriousness of the situation. Or all of the above, the box I checked all through high school.

That's it, I decide.

This has officially gone from terrifying to insane, I decide.

There's only one thing to be done, I decide.

I go downstairs.

It sounds like chanting. Like a Gregorian recording being played backwards. The din of the zombies moans is low—a haphazard choir they are clearly unaware of. The female is in one cell, and the males all corralled into another. Upon seeing me all of their arms, which were heretofore by their sides, go up like those action figure arms do when you press the button in the back. They all teeter-totter forward, and said arms slip between the bars, grasping at me somewhat lethargically. Furthermore, their collective moan barely raises a register.

Why are they so...well...subdued? There's really no other word for it. While they are not necessarily snoozing—and not just because the undead don't need shuteye—they aren't necessarily climbing the walls, either. Again, not just because they are incapable. My appearance has sparked considerable interest, but even so their response is not of the spastic variety.

That's when I see it. On the floor of the "male" cell. A human arm.

They...are...being...fed.

And then, he is behind me, hand on my shoulder, firm, angry. I spin around, my excuse at the ready, even while I'd prefer to inquire as to what *he* is doing.

"I just wanted to see them, to see what we're up against..." I begin. For the first time in my entire life I actually wonder where my anger is. Something, somewhere along the way worked; there is a hiding place, a door it is able to close and perhaps even lock.

But, it's not Letch or even his deputy, Nate. It's Smack. And he's too busy looking at the confined aberrations himself, equally perplexed.

"Letch is feeding them?" He can't take his eyes off of them. I can't blame him. This is the best way to describe a zombie:

1) Devoid of color—not even blue; they are cadaverously white. Which, okay, *is* a color, I guess.

2) Their eyes sprawl around the sockets in the same manner as a person *preparing* to die (as opposed to being dead already); I should know—I watched both of my parents draw their final breaths. One can be aimed straight up while the other vacillates from left to right, frantically. They spin like pinballs, yet can be focused directly upon you should they decide to feed.

3) Stiff. Frankenstein stiff, even when they move. Their elbows cease working, as do their knees, even though the latter retains, I'd say, 85% or so workability.

4) Three-dimensional bones. It's as if every bone in a zombie's body clammers to escape its confines, pressing against the flesh, stretching it like a beaten bed-sheet on a hotel mattress—and some of the bones break the skin.

5) The moan—constant, guttural, like kids on a roller coaster; it never stops, picks up as the cart nears the top, and turns into a full-on scream upon decline, i.e. attack. It's the sound of something or someone missing the ability to speak, accompanied by the frustration of not being able to say so.

"Yep. Yep, he is indeed feeding them."

Letch and his deputy have joined us downstairs, and the deputy is a percussionist as he confirms Smack's suspicion, jangling the many keys on the barracks' big ring. He hoists one up, caresses it even, running his thumb along the grooves. I can't help but pay heed, and neither can Smack. What are these guys truly up to?

"You guys are perfect," Letch adds, before either of us can say anything. "Ain't they?"

Nate laughs and nods. Takes his stun gun out.

Subdues a zombie, through the bars, evidently just for kicks, because he can, which is the bully's mantra. Or maybe simply to *show us* that he can, the control he has—they have—over them, and us, and pretty much everything. Probably did it for both those reasons.

"I've never been perfect for anything my whole life," I tell Letch, careful as I take a step back. The quarters are so narrow, I am concerned about being within a zombie's grasp if I move even one inch, so my step is clumsy.

"There it is. That—whadda they call it...that thing all you morning radio guys do. Puttin' yourself down." Letch searches his estimable mind, even if his vocabulary doesn't match up.

"Self-deprecation," Ivan suggests, from behind Letch, shotgun aimed square at his head. He cocks it.

"Right, right," concedes Letch, turning slowly, showing no sign of concern. "Self-deprecation. Even though they're arrogant motherfuckers, right? But, on the air they're just... normal folks. Like you and me.'" Letch says that last part sardonically, making quotation marks with his fingers. Ivan won't even allow a smile.

"You can go ahead and take a shot," adds Letch quickly. "My deputy dumped your ammo."

Ivan—in pure standoff mode and showing no sign of concern himself—aims the weapon over at a window and blows a hole through the glass. The sound is deafening and it sends the zombies into a tizzy.

"Shit!!" Nate shouts.

"Jesus Christ!" Letch barks, nostrils flaring. He looks over at his deputy, the anger on his face puffing the skins beneath his eyes; two volcanoes, his pupils bubbling, lava ready to blow and thrust two baby blues out at the man.

"Now, now," Ivan says coolly. "Don't blame Fife. You don't exactly ooze trust, Letch. I checked and promptly reloaded."

Letch's snort turns from an anger-fuelled one to a bemused one, and his guard goes down. Seemingly. "Gotta stop underestimating you, Ivan." Then— WHAM!—he tugs the rifle right outta Ivan's hands.

Shit is about to get ugly.

Letch aims the weapon back at its owner. "These two may be perfect. But you...you're so fuckin' expendable it's ridiculous." Ivan's arms—and jaw—are dropped. This is when Letch notices Ivan's war wound. And, much like when I noticed it—Ivan catches the registering of his zombie keepsake. Blinks his eyes slow, conveys acceptance of what can only be an immediate death sentence. But instead...

"Or maybe you're not," purrs Letch. "Well, how d'ya like that?"

"Hey. Fellas. While I don't necessarily disagree with you that I'm perfect, I have no idea what you're talking about. Or why we're all still down here with these things. Or why you're feeding 'em. Fact is, I don't even give a shit. I gotta get back to my lady." Smack is not doing that great a job of concealing his nervousness. He delivers this mini-monologue with the amount of conviction that might get him out of a bar fight, but only that much. Letch laughs in his face.

"I don't think she got the memo about being your lady," he says to Smack. Then, to his deputy: "Put 'em both in 'C'."

What follows is a lot of shouting, both human and inhuman (though the latter's unnerving howls can hardly

84

be constituted as shouts). Even so, I cannot differentiate between them and us by sound alone.

Smack and Ivan are doing a duet, with me sporadically chiming in—and the zombies that *haven't* been zapped into submission are supplying a *somnambulist* chorus. Amidst this chaos, both Letch and Nate (and by that I mostly mean Nate) manage to transfer the zapped zombie into "Cell C," along with Smack, who is backed in thanks to a repeated bumping of the end of Ivan's rifle—in Letch's hands—into his substantial chest. He makes no attempt to disarm Letch. It's like allowing someone to simply back you into a cage with a mountain lion with no resistance whatsoever; I get that it's the barrel of a shotgun you're staring down, but it's like the thought of that maybe being a more acceptable death doesn't even cross Gym Rat's mind.

It all happens ridiculously fast, like a movie catching you up to speed on things as the opening credits unravel. This is a Letch Production, no doubt about it. Ivan and I meagerly attempt to derail the abrupt incarceration, objecting, our body language speaking of a move to disarm them that never actually materializes. In other words, our bobbing and weaving is ignored, as are our objections, and, furthermore, our lack of understanding as to what exactly is happening doesn't necessarily help, either. This inability to comprehend and/or overcome our weapon-toting adversaries renders us merely the onlookers we are clearly intended to be.

Ya see, this is appearing to be a steel cage match. We're the audience. It's Smack versus zombie, the human clearly the underdog.

Smack doesn't get it until the deputy is closing the

cell door behind him. He first looks at me, with a "isn't he joining me?" expression. As Nate clicks the lock into place Smack's eyes bulge, hands gripping bars, white knuckles conveying desperation.

"What are you doing!? Let me out!" He can see that his pleas not only fall on deaf ears, but create a smile on the faces they're attached to. "I'll kill you!" He begins to shout. "I'll fucking kill you both!!"

"Gonna have ta kill him first." Letch points to Smack's zombie roommate, stirring in the corner, shaking off the daze caused by the taser and stun gun combo platter. A daze I didn't think a zombie could suffer.

Ivan, Smack, and I all seem to some to terms with what Letch is proposing at the same time, put the final piece of the puzzle into place at the exact same moment.

"You're crazy!" bellows Smack. "No way!" He is sweating profusely, knuckles ever whiter, forearms swollen with seething rage plus all-consuming fear. The zombie ambles towards him.

Letch tosses a knife into the cell, a smallish, beaten one with at least one whole roll of duct tape wrapped around its handle. Sucker's used for gutting fish at best. *Small* fish. It hits the floor with all the might of a snare drum at a pep rally.

"You sure about that?" Letch asks. The cell is barely the size of a walk-in closet, and the window of grabbing the knife before the zombie is on Smack is closing fast. "I'd really like to know."

I think Smack would, too. I know I would!

The other zombies are completely riled, invertebrate monkeys for the moment, the bones that have thus far so defined them seemingly dismantled as they bend backwards, wailing. Their groans are coming from so deep as to suggest internal bleeding being caused, with one snapping his thumb off upon thrusting his arm in between two bars. It hits the dank basement floor and bounces in front of me.

All this distracts me from Smack's predicament for a nanosecond. By the time I am looking back up at him he is kicking the zombie square in the chest, sending him reeling against the cement cell wall. Kickboxing 101.

Smack grabs the knife and begins waving it before the zombie, as if the undead can compute "West Side Story" theatrics. It reaches for him, nothing but stiff, rigid, albeit brittle bone, and Smack slashes his arm; the zombie does not even register the pain. In a way this a good thing, as it is not further infuriated by the gouge. This is the upside of zombie versus mountain lion: in battle a zombie cannot be *further* agitated, made angrier exponentially, due to a pain caused. They are at 10 at all times when in proximity of human flesh.

The downside, of course, is that a zombie will not flee in the face of that pain either, whimpering, off to find a place where it can lick its wounds. It keeps going and going and going. *The Energizer Zombie.*

Smack manages to land one more stab, and it's a good one at that: the zombie's throat. Alas, it is no more than an insect bite, and the creature is on him, knocking him over. Blood floods the cell floor, reaching out to Nate the deputy's feet.

"He's eating his face!" Nate shouts with a WWE glee.

"Let him out!" I shout. "There's still time to save him!!"

But they don't so much as move, save for Letch's

finger tapping the trigger of his firearm, still aimed squarely at Ivan.

"Rome's fuckin' burnin'," Ivan says softly. "Knew you were no good the second I saw you. Badge was like a fucking bicycle reflector."

"Take a good look," Letch replies, just as softly. "Ya see, Ivan...that's you and your protégée there in, oh, I'd say about a day."

"No," Ivan tells him firmly. "No, it ain't."

"Okay," allows Letch. "Good ol' Stan then. DJ boy'll come in handy as our announcer."

Before their spaghetti western exchange can continue something unexpected happens. Smack's scream transforms into a gurgle. And it might not even belong to Smack.

"I'll be damned!" the deputy exclaims, his left foot stomping in the puddle of blood he is standing in.

We all turn just in time to catch Smack finishing removing the zombie's head, the knife he jammed into its throat being thrust out the right side of its neck thanks to Smack's considerable forearm strength. The head rolls off and stops face up, the man it used to belong to long gone, its gaze finally joining him in the great beyond, down through cumulus or up through flame.

Chapter 10:
Up to Speed

Stan and Mary-Beth only knew of Mercedes from the tabloids, from supermarket check-outs and final stories on TV shows like "Entertainment Tonight" and "Inside Edition," just before their beloved "Wheel of Fortune" comes on. Her name may as well have been Escalade or Lexus.

Still, they stared. Not star-struck, but staring. To be fair, Mercedes does give off a vibe; she definitely has star quality.

They knew of the reality show debacle from Soap Opera Digest, Mary-Beth's "bible," Stan called it. They knew of her "relationship" with a heartthrob, of the whispers about rehab. Moreover, though, they stared simply because Mercedes was worth staring at. Even at a time like this, even with no make-up artist in sight, and the singer mid-fall from grace and looking like something the cat dragged in. Yes, even so. The cat had clearly dragged Mercedes in gently. She's a knockout.

Her delicate bone structure, flowing hair that defeated extension's purpose, and even the way she flipped that hair or moved her body: as if a god were her puppeteer. Not "the " God, but Zeus or some such.

"You're beautiful," Mary-Beth tells her, and not in a star-struck way, but more in an older woman to a younger woman acknowledging way.

"A beautiful disaster," Mercedes replies, but sweetly. "Thank you, though. Thank you so much."

She did not so much as raise an eyebrow at the aggressive way Smack was deposited back into their sleeping quarters. Nor did she seem to notice the quick once-over Nate gave him, a strip search with clothes still on, essentially a seeking of zombie markings.

"I'll be right outside," Nate says once he's satisfied. "All night."

With that he leaves. Mercedes still maintains an obliviousness to a turn of events that cannot help but to be noticed by both Stan and Mary-Beth.

Smack can only look at Mercedes in disbelief, her detachment to his beleaguered appearance—nay, complete and utter unawareness of it—is both befuddling and exasperating. His eyes are like lasers on her, jaw agape, his breath still not even caught.

"Do you...um...mind my asking why we now have a personal guard?" Stan manages to inquire.

"Because...!" blasts Smack. But then, thinking better, he takes it down a notch. "Because they just want to be safe. Make sure we're safe."

After all, why worry an older couple like Stan and Mary-Beth, the former an amiable, if bearish, new grandpa-type, and the latter a sweet-natured, well, new grandma-type—the new no doubt no longer applicable, as the dead burrowing up from their rotted caskets have seen to it that Connecticut's population dropped considerably in the past few days? Well, technically, there was a surge, what with their return and all, but you know what I mean.

In any event, why kick the shock into overdrive, add another layer of terror? I can see Smack coming to this conclusion, a new admiration of him, an absolute awe. Besides, how to relay what we've discovered, that, in addition to zombies being held captive downstairs, their captors are keen on playing Roman Coliseum and having humans take them on as if they are lions? Me, the court jester.

Smack sits besides Mercedes, catches his breath, or tries to anyway. One significant exhale cannot help but to get her attention.

"Are you all right?" she finally asks, eyes glassy. She is looking right at him. How she can do that and still ask the question has to be infuriating Smack.

"You mean," he whispers, "outside of just having to fight a zombie in one of the cells downstairs?"

"They're loose?" she asks, aping his whisper. He is confused, cannot make out what dots she just connected, how she got there, even while it does make total sense. Then he peers deeply into her eyes, and sees what I have already taken note of: Her pupils are dilated.

"No. They're not loose," he tells her, sighing. He has been here before. Mercedes is SO "been there, done that." Just...without the "done that" part, really. "Jesus, Cedes, what kind of pharmaceutical cocktail did you guzzle while I was fighting for my life with something that isn't alive?"

This question whizzes by her like a freight train.

91

"Wha...?" She laughs, and it is a sad mixture of confusion, being wasted, and post-traumatic stress. "What's that supposed to mean?"

"It means we're in deeper shit than we originally thought and here you are doubling up on your tabs."

"Running out is more like it. And fuck you, Smack. It's the end of the goddamned world. We need to loot every CVS and Rite-Aid from here 'til Kingdom Come. Which is where we're headed anyway. Don't get all holier than thou."

Mercedes flips her hair. She's got bags under eyes that wouldn't fit into the overhead compartment of a 747. She's a mess. This is where Smack decides he'll take whacked out over strung out. In other words, he keeps the meds coming. She holds out her hand, he digs into a pocket and hands her a pill.

Through the window of the office door we can both see Letch's number one man, good ol' Nate, carrying himself as if someone's going to make a break for it, a living, breathing ten-hut.

Then again, with the way Smack handled himself in the cell with that zombie, I don't blame him for staying on top of his game. Smack looks to be ruminating various ways of escape right about now, too, and I bet they all include—require, in fact—Zom-B. Oh yeah, I'm doing the first person thang.

Suddenly, as if Nate is telepathic, he calls me out, sticks me back with Ivan. I now get to shack up with him and even Letch himself. And a Q&A is not only not off limits, it is solicited by Letch.

"So," he begins, the control he feels infusing the tiny word, "don't just give the cat your tongue, boys.

Especially you, radio man, and when a zombie's probably gonna eat it like it's taffy any day now. If you're wondering what I'm up to, go ahead and ask away." He is rocking back and forth on an ancient wooden chair, and the creaking sound it makes rivals his gravelly voice in the grating department. He's got one eye on the window, focused on the empty state highway and into the woods that surround it, and the other, in a purely peripheral capacity, on the weapon he's fairly certain Ivan will lunge for at any second.

But, if you ask me, that's the last thing Ivan is thinking about. Right now anyway.

"I'll take you up on that," Ivan tells him. "I've got a question."

"Just one?"

"More of an observation, really."

"Do tell."

I can only sit and watch, a radio personality reduced to bystander status. Always a bitter pill. However, fact is, I have no questions, and I sure as hell haven't made any observations, either.

"Your, uh, female doornail down there," Ivan begins, pacing himself, more intense than he has been thus far.

"Uh huh?"

"She's got her own cell, and all the male undead are sharing space." Letch can only nod along at this point. But he does not look lost or in any way like he cannot imagine what Ivan is getting at. That much I do observe. "That's mighty courteous of ya."

"Uh huh." Letch says it this time with a Southern gentleman quality, neither of which he can claim.

"But, courtesy probably ain't the reason behind the

93

private quarters," Ivan continues. "Now, near as I can tell, there ain't a decayed sexual bone in their bodies, so you're not sparing her from some zombie gang bang."

Letch leans forward now, appears slightly antagonized. He chews slowly on the inside of his mouth, four to six teeth clamping down on the underbelly of his cheek, that longish front one protruding more than ever.

"No. No, I'm not," Letch confirms. "No, *we're* not. My deputy and I, I mean."

"Right. Your deputy and you," Ivan repeats, with a delivery that infers that the deputy is no more than a lap dog, about as much a voice in the decision-making going on as any of us have been or are going to be from this point on. Just an armed lap dog. "But, her pants...they're being kept up with a makeshift belt. Rope, far as I can tell. They've been pulled down and tugged off more than the sail of a boat at high sea during a hurricane."

Letch shifts his entire body back, as if to suggest he is appalled as to what Ivan may or may not be suggesting. He sprays his hands open, palms up, like the police—which he is—have weapons aimed at him. "Whoa," he says, mockingly.

"'Whoa.' *Please.* You gonna tell me a zombie had her wits about her enough to come up with a twine belt?" To this Letch has no immediate response. "Now, I know you thought, at best, one of us would ask what your thought process here is, why you're locking these suckers up, never mind getting a hard-on over steel-cage matches with humans. Fact is, that part I get. Even if it's just me. But, banging a zombie—that part I don't get. I ain't surprised, make no mistake, but I don't get it. You're like the kid in the neighborhood who shoved firecrackers up a stray cat's ass and wondered why we all didn't laugh our asses off. I was never him. And I never liked him."

"I don't know what you're talking about," Letch says, and in an abrupt manner that suggests he was about to say something else entirely, but changed his mind at the last second. "Maybe you can ask her what's up with her belt when you're one of 'em. How is that ol' arm anyway, Ivan?"

Letch grabs it, even while Ivan attempts to pull it free; they are at a stand-off, and it's obvious neither is necessarily stronger than the other.

"Don't worry about my arm," Ivan staunchly suggests.

"Guys, guys..." I interject. "This isn't getting us anywhere."

"Hmm," is all Letch says. Then, to me: "Well, we aren't going anywhere anyway, Wolfman Jack. 'Cept to hell. Right along with these fuckers." With that Letch lets go and heads for the door. He opens it, and then looks back at us both before departing: "May as well have some fun along the way."

95

Chapter 11:
Overnights

"I used to do overnights." Ivan's voice is low, raspy, breaking a silence the way a bumblebee entering a house through a hole in a screen window does. Is his tenor due to the fact that neither of us has said a word since Letch left us to our own devices? Or because he had, albeit briefly, fallen asleep and has just woken up? Or—oh, I dunno—because this is his zombie voice screen emerging, slowly but surely? One can only obsess. Oops, I mean guess. "Remember when there was a real, live person on the radio at three in the morning?"

"Remember when there were real, live people?" I counter.

He laughs. "My radio name was Eddie Steel. The saddest fucking people used to call in. This was before cell phones, of course."

"Of course," I concur. 'Cuz that's what you do with a soon-to-be-zombie, even while you're well aware there will be zero recollection.

97

"No drunk-dialing from the car on the way home from a club," he continues. "Just lonely-ass people. I'd stay on with them forever, as long as they wanted to. You wanted a call so bad during the overnight shift. I'd roll tape, cut it up three times, give some sobbing high school sophomore three different names just to make it look like more people were listening than there really were."

That pin drops. You know the one.

"Lotta lonely people in the world," Ivan adds. As if I didn't know, wasn't one of 'em even.

Beneath us, barely ten steps down, a prison cell full of zombies rattles and hums, cacophonous, a plugged-in bass guitar leaning on an amplifier, and the thought of them feeding on one another springs to mind. Why won't they? Why *don't* they? Humans would. We have. Put us on a snowcapped mountaintop, twenty feet from the remains of an airplane and without any food for three days tops and we dine on each other. What, zombies consider cannibalism beneath them?

"Tell me about the girl," Ivan says next, plucking me from yet another inner dialogue digression. Typically only prone to open up when the radio phone lines are also open, the darkness—and no doubt the situation—compels me to confide.

"What's to tell? She hates me. Can't say as I blame her. I took potshots every time she wound up in the news. We argued on the air and I got emails about it for months so I had to exploit it, make it seem like a 'feud' was in full effect. But, I actually like some of her stuff. And, damn, she's gorgeous. In an earthy way..."

"Hey. Shakespeare. I don't mean Mercedes," interrupts Ivan. "And did you really just use the word earthy?"

"You know what I mean. She's real. Grounded."

"Don't talk about ground while zombies are climbing out of it, asshole," jokes Ivan. Or, at least, I think he's joking. "I'm talking about the girl who died during your stupid radio stunt."

Another pin.

Karen Wildman. Mother of two. Happily married housewife. Her face haunted my dreams for maybe two years straight, and still makes cameos—or, at least, the photo of her that the local newspaper and TV news outlets ran ad nauseam throughout her dying during a stunt on the radio show that bore my name and subsequent funeral, firing, and lawsuit. What's worse, she entered the contest to win tickets to a teeny-bopper concert for said children, Tyler and Annabelle. They pop up from time to time, too. So does the crucifix tattoo on her arm, which was such a contradiction to her otherwise plain-Jane, soccer mom look. What kind of declaration was this anyway? I see that tattoo, in my dreams, dancing while her tendons tensed in accordance to our silly little radio stunt, push-ups, chin-ups, jumping jacks—our ridiculous "Survivor" reality show rip-off contest. One night, Karen's auburn bob burst into flame in a particularly disturbing nightmare—not that the others were any less disturbing, just not as F/X-laden.

"*Girl,*" I repeat, Ivan's clarification hanging in the dark area between us in stark contrast to the one I am making now. "Try mother. That's why I didn't know who you meant—the word girl in reference to her somehow...I dunno...it stings more."

"Christ, kid...it wasn't your fault. It was a radio station stunt. She signed the disclaimer, didn't she? There was a nurse on hand that day, no? At the event? Damn, it was 95 degrees out, if I remember right."

"Sounds like you know all there is to know," I say, the height of indignant. I mean, why prod me to "tell him about the girl" if he knows so Goddamned much?

I hear him stir. He may be sitting up. "Ya don't have to get all emotional, Zom-B." He says my radio name mockingly. How could he not? "Don't carry that around with you, especially now. I guess I was just wondering if there was anything more to the story. More than those of us in the business in this stinkin' state know anyway. 'Cuz there usually is."

"Just that I never wanted to do the stupid stunt in the first place, maybe. But, I never spoke up. Never said a word, man. Been getting paid to speak almost my entire adult life and I didn't at probably the most important time."

Ivan gets his own pin.

The halcyon days of radio. I recall the first time I my program director and I made the rounds in New York City, from record label to record label, and from "in-store" to "in-store" (that's when artists sing and sign copies of their new release at record stores or bookstores). I met one artist long since been and gone, that year's Mercedes, really, though a semi-bluesy rocker.

The station had a limo take us both straight from Connecticut to Fifth Ave, champagne and mini-recorder in tow. (The latter because, delusional cat that I was I figured I would leave with an interview that would land on MTV's desk, wherein they would decide that despite my less-than-photogenic looks I was going to be their next

VJ-cum-late night TV host.)

The entire drive there my PD (acronym for program director) sounded like Charlie Brown's parents; his words took no shape, had no meaning, as I truncated his war stories (at best) in favor of reverie. I was quite certain this trip would be like nothing I'd experienced thus far and, in truth it wasn't. Not by a long shot.

We hit a label first, where we were to meet some execs, pile them into our limo, smoke weed or do lines, and then catch the first in-store. I expected a hustling, bustling office where eager young executives played Nerf football while they spouted off ideologies and marketing strategies for their artists, where knockouts prowled the hallways on six-inch heels, catching the eye of rock stars as they coordinated their itineraries, where deals were sealed and wounds were healed.

But it was decidedly different than that. Loud, yes; full of hustle and bustle, yes; itineraries coordinated, yes. Yes to it all, really, but devoid of genuine enthusiasm. The thousand dollar power suits and skirts may as well have been on conveyor belts: the stiff denizens off the Delancey Street subway line couldn't manage a smile for fear of a wrinkle they'd have to eventually Botox away. Since so many of them were fifteen or so.

I kept hearing the same two words, too: "I'm psyched." Yet not one soul who ever uttered them actually appeared to be psyched. Their high-fives were constant, spasm-like, as if this act was the entire first day of orientation.

When I met bluesy rocker I mentioned she appeared either equally disappointed and disillusioned or as if she were drinking from the same fountain of monotone

101

boorishness. Her rep delivered ushered her in and announced her latest single just "cracked the Top 40 with a bullet."

"How does that make you feel?" I asked straightaway, well aware of the ubiquity of that question to a recording artist but adhering to its necessity nonetheless.

"I love my fans," the Stepford Wife replied.

And it was I who was now wishing for a bullet—in my head.

Chapter 12:
Mourning Show

Letch wakes both Ivan and I with the barrel of his rifle, poking Ivan significantly harder and from a more defensive stance, not entirely sure how the disgruntled engineer may rise—meaning human versus inhuman. Or formerly human. Or semi-zombie. Aw, you know what I mean.

He seemed somewhat surprised when Ivan merely rubbed his eyes, coughed the morning cough of a man who has smoked nearly his entire life, and shouted, "Boo!"

But, I was the truly surprised one when Letch informed us that we had one more broadcast to put in the can before we left for Niantic.

"Huh?"

"You heard right, *Zom-B*." No one seems capable of saying the name without some sort of sardonic inflection or tweaked pronunciation at this point, and I can't say as I blame 'em. "You're the voice of the survivors is what you are. A powerful position."

"Not when there's a gun aimed at you," I inform him.

"Shit, the FCC ain't a gun?" he asks facetiously.

"And what exactly will I be relaying?"

"You're gonna tell whoever may be left out there with a heartbeat where to go so we can all meet up. And the ones who are in remotely good shape get to fight doornails to the death." Ivan lights up a cigarette stub. He knows he's right, and I do too. Now that he's spelled it out so succinctly even more so.

"But you're leaving out the most important part!" declares a wide-eyed and somehow well-rested Letch. "That you'll be the emcee"—he points at me (of course)—"and that our halftime performer is none other than hit recording artist Mercedes!"

As if on cue Nate bursts through the door, his right fist firmly wrapped around what Mercedes is passing off as a wrist. He even announces their arrival via a ridiculously over-the-top "Ta-Da!" I see Smack brooding in the background and my eyes trail down from his intense stare to where his own wrist is handcuffed to a radiator. We convey to one another with pointed pupils our helplessness, our haplessness; ditto a desire to hatch some sort of scheme, some sort of way out of this mess.

While I obviously cannot read his mind, or therefore speak for him, I can say this much with a degree of confidence: We would rather die at the hands of the undead than at the hands of the depraved.

Mercedes is in a zombie state of her own. "What's happening?" she manages weakly. She looks like she didn't get even a second of sleep, and I can't say that I bested her in that regard—not much anyway. Ivan, however, managed to not only grab a few hours, but drown out the din of the zombies below with his stentorian snoring. I look Mercedes directly in the eyes but cannot seem to penetrate. The bags beneath them have doubled in size, and her ribs can be seen through that thin designer T-shirt. She wouldn't be much of a meal for the undead, a plate returned to the kitchen at the Zombie Diner.

"It's all right, honey," Ivan assures Mercedes, this paternal, nurturing vibe appearing for the first time. It's touching, really.

"That's touching. Really." Letch then spits onto the hardwood floor and follows that mockery with, "Now let's go make some of that radio magic!"

All of us—Stan, Mary-Beth, a handcuffed Smack, Mercedes, Ivan, and I—are assembled into the broadcast office, sans continental breakfast. It's barely 7 a.m. Letch is guzzling iced coffee, which is really just coffee grinds stirred vigorously in a Dixie cup of water, as is Nate. Nate's face suggests it is not all that tasty, but Letch doesn't even seem to register how unpalatable it is. Nor does he seem to register the same with regard to his actions, or the "Death Match" he is in the throes of organizing, though.

"Undead Match," he says, just as I am thinking all of this. "That's what I want you to refer to it as, deejay boy."

"And who am I broadcasting to, might I ask?"

"Anybody who might be left. Hell, look what your last broadcast dragged in!" Letch points at Mercedes, Smack right by her side, seething, hands now cuffed behind his back. "Tell everyone who's looking to survive this madness to head to the casino. That's the meeting place."

"But I thought we were headed to Niantic today?" Stan says meekly. He still doesn't seem to get everything that's going on, which is unquestionably a good thing.

"Just doing a pick-up there," Nate tells him. "The prison."

"Oh, great, then there are others," Mary-Beth adds.

"You can say that," Nate tells her.

"Alright, cue 'er up," Letch commands Ivan, who can only comply.

Ivan doesn't really do much of anything, but even so dramatically announces, "Ready when you are," to me. That tells me this segment we're laying down is going to have an intro, and we just recorded it. In short, *he was already rolling tape.*

"Hello survivors," I begin. Letch plops his hand over the microphone.

"More energy," he instructs. "More urgency."

"Well, this is an urgent situation simply as it stands, wouldn't you say?" I counter. He grits his teeth, and I hear them screeching across one another, especially that longish one, similar to fingernails on a chalkboard.

I begin again. With more energy. "Survivors! This is Luke Z, DJ Zom-B, for those of you who may recognize that name. I apologize for the insensitivity of it now. I actually apologize for it in general. God, that's a stupid name. Imagine if Wolfman Jack was still alive and we were being attacked by werewolves, though. How stupid would HE feel?"

Everyone looks at me curiously, and I begin to feel like a real idiot for this random hypothetical. But, then I hear something quite interesting. One person giggling.

Mercedes. I smile at her. She looks at me differently than she ever has before.

"Okay, anyway, listen up," I continue, deejay oomph infusing my delivery. "There are still some of us left. You are NOT alone. We are all heading to the casino. If you hear this, if you are mobile, please head there." I look over to Letch and shrug my shoulders, wondering if I've said enough, said it all to his liking. He points at Mercedes.

"The beautiful and talented singer Mercedes has survived and is with us," I add. I feel like an idiot again, which I basically have my entire life anyway. Ya know, you really don't get used to it, comfortable with it. The way I announce her being with us is the only manner in which I am comfortable. I will not announce a performance. But I do follow that with: "Surely that's a silver lining." She smiles back. It looks like there hasn't been one on her face in a while, and as if she barely has the strength or wherewithal TO smile, but she does, so there ya go.

Ivan clicks the recorder off.

"Well, wasn't that sweet?" taunts Letch. "Good job, deejay boy. A'right, listen up! Everyone out, single file, to the two vehicles. My deputy has already loaded in the undead portion of our carpool, so you're safe. Ivan, transmit that sucker."

Ivan begins to punch in codes, but is doing so in a less than confident capacity, and finally presses the "cancel" button, which both Letch and I cannot help but to notice, even while I am watching Mercedes wander out the door, directly in front of Smack, gun to her head to keep him in line.

"Forget the code already? After two freakin'

transmissions? Christ, Ivan."

"Did you EVER know it?" Ivan fires back, much to Letch's surprise. His eyes go wide, but he pauses, takes a breath, rather than replying with the butt of his weapon being pole-vaulted into Ivan's paunch.

"Um, no, Ivan, I didn't. I was out on the highways, chasing down rapist scumbags or playing chicken in the wrong lane with a privileged Connecticut runt in his father's sports car, high on some drug they give to ele-fuckin'-phants."

"Understood," Ivan says indifferently. "Lemme look up the code again. My brain is fried."

"Well," Letch suggests, "the brain is the first thing to go considering what's happening to you."

I actually think Letch is correct in this assessment but Ivan shoots him a look that suggests he is completely puzzled by the remark. I wonder how much time "Ivan" can possibly be left. I've been with him for 24 hours alone. Can the transformation from human to subhuman seriously take much longer?

"Got it." Ivan punches in some numbers and presses "Send."

"Good man. Let's go." Letch walks over to the door and waves his weapon for us to exit before he does. Upon reaching the hallway he aims said weapon at some cases on the floor. "Each of you grab one of those." It bottled water, 24 per box.

"Mighty generous of you," Ivan tells Letch sarcastically. He's back.

Suddenly, there is a beeping sound being emitted by the EAS. Neither Ivan nor myself make a move to check on it, both afraid to make *any* sudden moves, very much in prisoner mode, despite not being handcuffed.

"Shit, what the fuck is wrong now? Ivan, if you're fucking up on purpose...!" Letch's eyes are black, pure sadism, less human than even the zombie eyes I've looked into.

I am the closest to the system. I peer over and report, "It says 'Sent.' It's just saying the broadcast was successful."

"Oh," hiccups Letch. "Good." He then places another case of bottled water on top of the one already in my hands. "Let's hit the road, boys."

We file out, one by one, into a blinding morning sun, both the tour bus and the paddy wagon awaiting and idling; I wonder if I will ever be idle again, how much time I spent in my life being exactly that, and laugh to myself at yet more irony.

Then I wonder about what I really saw flashing on the EAS console, as the word "Sent" wasn't it; that was a lie. What I actually saw flashing was one number followed by three letters: *4.) NIC.*

What the hell did Ivan just do?

Chapter 13: Daytrippers

Being inside Mercedes tour bus is a trip. There's no way I was going to see the inside of this thing otherwise, not even in an interviewing capacity. And her new record definitely needed the help.

There are empty spaces in the overhead compartments where high-end DVD players and stereo equipment used to be, and the gaping hole where a huge flat screen TV used to sit has a set a third the size plunked inside it, reeking of reprimand; when she turns it on it might even have her dead Crunch exec's voice on a constant loop asking, "Where's the single? Where's the single?" The whole interior smacks of downgrade, save for...well... Smack.

Smack had been earning a nice name for himself in the industry. His sticking with Mercedes obviously spoke of his character, too. But character can be sand in the gas tank of the recording biz. He co-produced a few other artist's records and co-wrote Pink's last album, the whole shebang. He was being sought out.

The tabloids were painting him with the spurned lover brush as Mercedes paraded around town with dreamboat Chad Bawling, but I think you have to have been a love to ever be a spurned one, right? Mercedes kept playing the oblivious card, too, when asked about Smack in interviews. How many times can a gal reply, "What!?" or "Ya think?" incredulously? After at least a half dozen one interviewer would have to get one "I keep hearing that," or so you'd think.

In any event, Mercedes tour bus is as bleak as the city streets. All three seasons of "Drama Queen" sit on an empty shelf with no DVD player to watch Chad Bawling on. Shrink wrap still on.

"I don't understand what's happening," Mary-Beth keeps saying.

"Hush," Stan keeps saying immediately afterwards.

Smack is struggling to find one iota of comfort in sitting while handcuffed, again with his eyes to me as if we're in this together. Which, obviously, we are. He's trying to reach his upper chest with his chin, ostensibly due to an itch. Mercedes is looking at him cross-eyed, like she thinks he is suffering from some sort of spasm, her obliviousness knowing no bounds. Selective obliviousness I like to call it, and it manages to remind me of my three-week high school devastation even all these years later. Pathetic.

Finally, Smack gives up, a massive sigh escaping— escaping something none of us will probably do in the pure sense. He looks at Mercedes, exasperated, veins in his neck bulging. That's when she does it.

She smiles, just getting it, and raises her hand slowly,

the half dozen bracelets and all the rings, the bling, the ring-a-ding having been removed, her wrist and fingers naked, the skin on two knuckles scraped via what must've been an abrupt, frustrated removal process. Maybe they were even flung against something. Her fingers reach Smack, directly beneath his chin and she begins to scratch softly. He cranes his neck so she can reach the spot demanding the most attention. Only thing missing is thumping his leg in doggie thanks.

For whatever reason this is equal parts heart-warming and heart-breaking.

"I don't understand what's happening."

"Hush."

Letch is behind the wheel, while Nate follows us in the paddy wagon. Who or what is waiting for us in Niantic is anyone's guess. More zombies, definitely. More police, definitely. More humans, I'm not so sure. It's this last part that is the most dismaying, for if we are the only ones left, and no one responds to my last broadcast, then Smack and Stan have some undead matches awaiting them. How long before Mercedes and I have to follow, the "talent" notwithstanding?

I look over at Ivan. Despite a haphazard five o'clock shadow and considerable soiling of his clothes due to perspiration, urinary discharge (involuntary or not), and scuffle, he is none the worse for wear. Meaning, this zombie transformation of his is taking its own sweet time. Lucky for us I guess. It's just, I woulda thought that kinda thing happened within twenty-four hours. Of course, we're not far outside of that amount of time, which causes more dismay, but it's a dismay I've become accustomed to.

"Hey, Ivan," I say softly. He turns to look at me, his eyes heavy, lids swollen from rubbing, and with fingers the size of bratwursts. "You gonna tell me what that 'NIC' on the EAS screen stood for?"

"Hush."

I was once carted off to the local jailhouse for a barroom brawl—a good old-fashioned free-for-all wherein bottles flew, jukebox hiccupped, elbows met unintended throats, and the catalyst was something no one could quite recall when questioned. There mighta been a girl involved, or a spilt drink, or an overheard insult, or—yet again—D.) All of the above.

What everyone could agree on, however, was that I had thrown the first punch. I missed...by a mile...but I still threw it.

As all six of us—me and my two friends, and the three complete strangers we fought—were all taken downtown in the paddy wagon we sat there in silence. The lone sound heard the entire three minute ride, as we weren't far for the jailhouse, especially considering most jailhouses are not far from any city's thriving club district, was someone's tooth hitting the floor. And maybe a few moans and groans.

We were bloodied, beaten, and soon to be bailed out. Not one word was uttered, not even from friend to friend.

A police station at two in the morning is quite the experience. Particularly on the weekends. Fuck that "must be a full moon" rhetoric, too; that just gives people an excuse.

The guy behind the desk—the anchor, if you will—was hands down the most puzzling police officer in the place.

Screaming, clawing, crying, drunken, cracked out folks were brought before him and he didn't so much as raise an eyebrow. One, I swear, dripped blood on the countertop maybe two inches away from where he was reading the newspaper and, without even taking his eyes off the uber-challenging Jumble, he reached under the counter, grabbed some cleaner, sprayed the splatter, reached back down, wiped, and then jotted in a word.

"Detach," he said aloud. Triumph.

The seated officers took their own sweet time when it came to answering the phone, third and fourth ring, and they were just staring at stacks of paperwork, maybe leafing, no writing, feet crossed and gingerly placed on flipped over wastepaper baskets. No ruckus disturbed them, garnered their wrath, never mind their attention.

Not the slurring prostitute.

Not the belligerent frat boy.

Not the resisting-arrest crack addict.

Not the namedropping dealer.

Not even the fingernails-like-switchblades frenzied ex-girlfriend who clawed one officer's face as she screamed about him "feeling her up and not frisking her."

Even that officer merely cuffed her robotically, tended to his wound, and left booking her up to his partner while he caught the "Saturday Night Live" cast saying goodbye, hugging each other and prancing and preening.

In fact, all of the officers wheeling degenerates, lowlifes, and everything else in and out did so in a conveyor belt capacity, stoic yet forceful, business as usual, dropping one off and then being told about more domestic disputes or disorderly conduct and thus promptly dispatched. It was as if someone were behind the scenes,

working all of them with a joystick, "Grand Theft Auto" before "Grand Theft Auto" existed.
   The game I mean.

"I don't understand what's happening."
"Hush."
"No. I won't hush. I won't!" Mary-Beth is becoming unglued. "You! Driving! Where are you taking us? Why are you taking them with us?"

Stan looks at Ivan and I as if he's in on everything with us, as if he's seen what we've seen, knows everything there is to know when, fact is, I am fairly certain I don't even know that. This is the list of things that I know but Stan does not:

1) Connecticut is being lopped off from the rest of the United States (along with two, maybe three other states—at this point), left completely for dead.

2) Letch plans on spending whatever time he has left squaring the humans off against the zombies, for his own sadistic enjoyment, in a psycho riff on the Roman Coliseum.

3) Ivan will be fighting for the other team.

* * * * *

I have never met Stan before, so I cannot attest as to how swift he is, how adept at gleaning things from stolen glances, half sentences, and sadistic stares he may be or, furthermore, how clueless he may be to same. Maybe he does have an idea, but isn't letting on, particularly for his increasingly frazzled wife's sake. Even if he does, though, he cannot possibly know all of what I just listed. Just as I am more than likely oblivious to much myself. This is a list of things I may not know:

1) Letch is acting in accordance with directives from a superior, perhaps even someone outside the state.

2) "United Fates" is the work of the United States government.

3) The President is a zombie.

"There! There!" Mary-Beth continues, though now frantically pointing at a highway rest area. "Why aren't we at least stopping for food!? There's an abandoned McDonald's! Aren't you thinking about food at all? What kind of plan is this!?"

"Ya know what?" Letch begins. I see Stan grab his wife's hand, squeeze it, bracing himself, a steel, married, senior brace—the kind I'd imagine equates to the stuff of last stands. "She's right."

Letch turns the signal light on and gets Nate's attention by leaning heavily on the horn. McDonald's, here we come.

"Omigod," gushes Mercedes. She locks eyes with Mary-Beth, a childlike exuberance taking over. She has just shed six or seven years before my very eyes or, maybe more so, simply revealed just how young she really is. "Thank you *so much*."

Visions of cold Big Macs, chewy (albeit legendary)

117

French fries, soupy strawberry milkshakes, and whatever other goodies remind Mercedes of the childhood she swapped for stardom are obviously dancing in her head, and Mary-Beth, too, more than twice her age, has stopped squawking due to the food run.

Soon the door to the tour bus is opened. From the outside. (Nate couldn't have gotten much sleep, either, as the bus is rigged in a way that would make leaping out while Letch is driving impossible, with boards nailed over the tinted windows and the door boasting an apparatus not unlike ancient dungeons, slabs of wood slipped into steel trappings that can only be lifted outside the vehicle.) The sunlight rushes into the tour bus and blinds us all. Letch's voice is then heard.

"Place your orders, fellas."

"Huh?" Smack growls.

"This is girls only," Letch replies, and then looks directly at Mercedes. "Don't be all anorexic in there, honey. Grab everything you can carry. But, Stan the Man, if you got a favorite Mickey D's item, place your order. Then again, the Missus obviously knows it from probably a million McDonald's trips together."

"No way," Smack says firmly. "She's not going in there alone. *They're* not going in there alone."

"R-right," manages Stan. "Why can't we go with them?"

"Hero discouragement let's call it."

"You got it all figured out, don't you, officer?" I inquire. My patience is nearing its end, much like everyone else's. "I think I speak for everyone when I say that we'd prefer the zombies' company to yours."

I feel everyone's eyes on me, Ivan proud as a papa

118

and both Mercedes and Smack seeing me in a new light. But, they don't know me. I've got fifteen years on both of them. Fifteen years of troubles with the law, of world-weariness, of loss. You stop marking your territory with piss at my age, while Mercedes and definitely Smack are at the height of that nonsense.

"Soon enough, deejay boy," Letch responds. "My deputy is standing by the entrance to McDonald's. The ladies will be fine. You either want food or you don't."

* * * * *

Being let into an abandoned McDonald's—the ultimate teenager, stoner, pregnant woman, hungover person's dream. I'm sure it's many other people's dream, too, including starving post-apocalyptic zombie fighters, which is us, even if some of us don't know, but those four categories are probably the quintessential. Even if it has been several days since anything was prepared there, and even if what is left over is cold from days of sitting, and what occupies the refrigerator is either soured or on the brink of it. Fact is, no one arches an eyebrow at the Golden Arches, even at a time like this.

Mercedes and Mary-Beth stepped cautiously over broken glass to enter, through what used to be the front door. Nate was right behind them, eyes vacillating between the paddy wagon and the darkened fast food joint. He had done one quick sweep prior to letting them in and announced that the coast was clear. That was enough for both of them, and they tore in.

Mercedes immediately dumped a huge cardboard box of straws over, that she found beneath the counter, and placed it on top. She began frantically dumping items into it, like she was on one of those 60-second shopping sprees. What she was grabbing wasn't all that great, either: the packaged apples that come with the Happy Meal, handfuls of cold fries, and packages of condiments.

Mary-Beth on the other hand went right for where cold burgers sat under what used to be the heat lamp. However, rather than tossing them to her sidekick she began unwrapping and eating them, stuffing them into her mouth like a...well, zombie would a human lung.

"I worked at a McDonald's, ya know," Mercedes told her, unaware at this point that she wasn't gathering food but was instead eating it. "For one year, while I worked on a demo and dated a loser pot dealer." Catching herself, or thinking about who exactly she was sharing this with instead, Mercedes turned, embarrassed, which dissipated quickly upon finding Mary-Beth polishing off a Filet o' Fish. "What are you doing? Just put everything in a box. We'll eat on the bus."

"Oh," Mary-Beth said, the thought having never crossed her mind. She was in a McDonald's-induced coma. Mercedes looked out towards the bus just then, and the front door where Nate nervously paced. The zombies pounding on the door of the paddy wagon could be heard from behind the counter, and Mercedes fretted if that could act as a rallying cry for others.

"Here." Mercedes handed Mary-Beth a cardboard box, after dumping out the six different types of sugar packets inside. Then she grabbed a fistful and threw them in her picnic basket; she would gleefully down some Splenda at some point down the road, depending upon length of road. A sugar substitute that was considered more health conscious being offered at McDonald's is funny, really, but so, too, is the pop star on a steady diet of anxiety medication salivating over sugar packets. "Put all the sandwiches in there. And don't forget some nuggets!"

Mary-Beth did as she was told, slowly at first, emerging from the coma almost begrudgingly. Mercedes stumbled upon the cabinet where the infamous apple pies are kept. "Jackpot!" she shouted. (McDonald's apple pies can now be a post-apocalyptic delight, while the initial form they took—bubbling apple sauce encased in a deep-fried lard—probably would've spontaneously combusted, and if they didn't they still wouldn't be digestible. Or, at least, *enjoyably* digestible anyway.)

"Let's go, ladies!" Nate's anxiousness was getting the better of him, and why wouldn't it? How much pounding can the door of a paddy wagon take from a half dozen flailing zombie fists and probably even heads? Not much.

"On our way!" Mercedes declared energetically, and Mary-Beth was indeed in tow. Both of their boxes were overflowing.

"I'm so glad you mentioned the nuggets, honey," Mary-Beth told her. But, then she stopped dead in her tracks.

"What?" asked Mercedes. "What is it?"

"I forgot sauces," Mary-Beth answered, and then placed her box down and scrambled to the back, into the kitchen, deeper into the bowels of the fast food joint than either of them have been. Mercedes could hear doors opening and closing.

"Ah, don't worry about it," Mercedes bellowed. "I've got ketchup and mustard packs."

"Stan likes the barbecue sauce," Mary-Beth replied.

Then Mercedes heard another door being opened, the stainless steel elongated handle singing its tune. While she waited she looked down at the half-eaten Filet o' Fish on top of Mary-Beth's box and debated finishing it. Nah, she decided. That would be unrefined.

"We'd better go!" she instead yelled sweetly. "I'm sure Stan would rather you be back safe and sound than go on a wild goose chase for barbecue sauce."

"What's the hold-up?" Nate chimed in, leaning through the fractured door carefully.

"She's looking for the sauces for the nuggets."

"Je-sus Christ," he huffed. "Wait here."

Nate disappeared into the back, deftly, all back-to-the-wall antics and training stances on display. When he kicked open the door to the kitchen he found a zombie reaching into where Mary-Beth's face used to be, trying to extract her brain.

Nate gagged. Which was underscored by a stumbling syntax. "Oh...uh...ack...fuck!" He could vomit, felt it rushing up, the chips and chocolate from the vending machine at the state police barracks, all of it, along with the stench of the undead he'd convinced himself he'd gotten used to but totally hasn't.

The zombie turned, conveyed zombie frustration that it could not get the brain out of Mary-Beth's head. It had cracked the oyster shell and couldn't get the oyster, never mind a potential diamond. It lunged for Nate, as much as a zombie can lunge anyway.

Nate began firing rounds, but he was all over the place. Couldn't even hit what's right in front of him. The zombie got a hold of his arms and opened wide. It wanted another face, fingers like flu shots. Nate managed to get

122

his weapon just under the thing's neck and unloaded a round that split the undead head in half, the front falling off and onto the linoleum and the back staying in place for ten seconds or so, before it then fell off as well.

He ran off, certain the sound of ammunition being discharged could only result in calamity, from more zombies coming out of the woodwork (the witless cretins, unable to distinguish between what could spell food and what could spell death), to Letch leaving him high and dry.

On his way out he saw Mercedes frozen in her tracks, the shock she had just begun to shake back in spades. Surprisingly, Nate displayed sensitivity.

"Come on, girl," pleaded the deputy. "Don't freak out on me now. It's all good, I took care of it. Let's just get this stuff into your pretty bus there and be on our way." He gently nudged her, and even managed to grab Mary-Beth's box with one hand.

"W-where is...um...what was her name?"

"Damned if I knew her name either, honey. And saying she's in a better place wouldn't exactly be a lie."

As Nate and Mercedes stepped back out into the blinding sun, Mercedes lost without her Jackie O shades, never mind all the other accoutrements, trappings of a fame she was able to shed just about as quickly as she did her teenaged skin, Letch turned over the engine on the tour bus.

But, even as Letch gave it the gas, and the catalytic converter on the gas guzzler hacked and coughed, Stan could be heard wailing.

* * * * *

My court-ordered anger management classes are, sadly, irrefutably unusable here. I look at Stan, both seething and sobbing, fists clenched and looking like stitching, plus the word "Spalding" across them would not be out of place, a time bomb waiting to either ex or implode. I do, however, want to at least pass on what I learned from my time spent in there, despite the fact that they never truly "took"; I didn't mail it in, mind you—I took it all very seriously, but it wasn't all that remarkable or effective, or at least not as much as simply going numb. I try to recall the exercises, the mantras I was instructed to repeat to myself, the breathing patterns. But Stan looks as if he'd punch me in my face were I to try to pass it all on.

Tears stream down his swollen, reddened cheeks, his eyes bugged and darting. He looks like someone coming to and realizing a major organ has just been removed.

"This is fucked," Smack says, to no one and everyone. "This is all fucked." He is still cuffed, and veins push out against his T-shirt, like leaches have latched to his chest, his blood pumping almost visible.

"That just about sums it up," confirms Ivan.

I can only look at Stan. Stan is all that I see. I cannot endeavor to get all melodramatic and suggest that I "feel his pain," yet it is highly accurate to say that I feel woven into the fabric of that pain, unyielding in the face of it, like talking around it is not only seriously insensitive but something I may not even be capable of.

"Stan...? You with us?"

Ivan, Smack, and Mercedes all look at me like I'm poking a lion. Mercedes is sitting right next to him, her body heat upon him she is so close; her hand rests so lightly on his left shoulder that only potholes cause connection.

Ivan shoots me a look that screams "leave it alone." Simultaneously, Mercedes rises to come sit beside me, perhaps concluding that Stan would prefer to be left alone right now and not share his seat with anyone, even while the rest of us realize her proximity just might be the only thing keeping him in check. Smack watches her trek over to my booth in disbelief or, at least, that's what my peripheral vision tells me. He is nearing not being able to restrain his grunts territory.

"I'm worried about him," Mercedes all but whispers. Prior to all this I would not have thought her capable of such compassion. Prior to all this she might not have been.

"I'm worried about all of us," I counter.

She cocks her head sideways, reveals a sly smile that only I can see, something that suggests she is well aware that my concern for all of us, at this particular moment in time, pales in comparison to my concern for Stan, and that saying anything to the contrary is a waste of both of our time. I breathe for the first time in days. Her eyes, her smile, enable this.

"She was looking for his favorite sauce," adds Mercedes, looking away, talking even more softly. "I don't want to tell him that—I won't tell him that—but she went way in the back for him, to find something she thought would make this more bearable for him, and that's when it happened. He wouldn't want to hear that, would he?"

Would he?

Speculate is all that I can do. All of my years lived, all of the relationships that have come and gone, the loss and the highs and the lows and the radio shows, it cowers in the corner as I meditate on this. Fact is, what the fuck do I know?

Have I loved? I guess.

Have I lost? Sure.

Can I even begin to fathom the agony that Stan is attempting to cope with right now, or attempting to keep a lid on, really? No. Absolutely not. I traded all things real for a reel.

Mercedes is in the same boat, both of us simply having sailed different waters, her beginning out into the ocean and me never getting out of the mooring. But she traded it all too. We have much in common, even while she would surely think her and Smack had more. Maybe they do; again, what the fuck do I know?

She has pulled it together in her feeling for Stan, her focus on him and his pain dethroning her shock and sadness at all events leading up to the here, the lousy now.

"Did you...see anything?" I ask her, Stan only a few feet away, bristling, knocking on breakdown's door. Mercedes nods her head no.

Meantime, Letch has us careening down the highway, "Niantic Next Exit" on the sign that's coming at me like a right hook. He is directly behind Nate, who somehow managed to thrust Mercedes into the bus, along with goodies no one has touched, and simply said to Stan, "I'm sorry." That was all Stan got.

* * * * *

Letch pulls the tour bus in front of the prison and simultaneously turns on the stereo. The lugubrious, notorious first few notes register immediately.

"*Sweet Emotion*," I say. Then, to Mercedes: "Radio?"

"My mix," comes the reply. But, from Smack. "I made it for her."

"Not that shit rapper version, is it?" Ivan wonders aloud. The "outburst" succeeds in deflating the tension Smack's declaration managed to create, even while Stan continues to totter on the edge of his seat, bereft and inconsolable; somehow our musings about the music don't seem inappropriate. Maybe because they aren't.

"No," Smack informs Ivan, amidst grinning. "But Run DMC ruled."

"Album cut," I point out. "Nice. The radio edit is insulting."

Letch turns the music up. It is obvious his reasoning is to distract us from the "pick-up." It is almost to the point where we have to shout to hear one another.

"What's the Triple-A radio edit make the Aerosmith classic anyway? Two minutes long?" Smack asks.

He's teasing. It's amazing that we can even be there, not just due to our relationship but the circumstances.

"Two and a half."

"You nailed the song, like, from the first note," Mercedes remarks. "All the morning guys I met over the past few years don't even seem to like music."

"The salespeople in radio like the music more than the jocks," I tell her. "And I nailed it in the first note because it was one of the first songs I played on guitar. Plus, because my high school girlfriend and I used to...um...listen to Aerosmith a lot."

"Ah," says Mercedes. "Thanks for the picture. That's an interesting observation about the salespeople in radio, too. What's that all about?"

"The observation's more about the jocks, all of whom seemed to be on the same pathetic page. That the radio station they're at is just a stepping-stone. How many times I heard those words: Stepping-stone. Ugh. They're all TV game show hosts or reality show hosts biding their time evidently."

"That explains a lot. Doesn't it, Smack?"

"Well, that wasn't really something I needed spelled out for me," growls Smack.

"That seems like another life anyway." I can see her saying the words, her lips like a beautiful, flawless cursive. I nod along in agreement, and she watches me do so. Me playing it in a band was one life, and playing it on the radio another, and the one with my ex-girlfriend yet another. Smack can only continue to fidget and watch in dismay as Mercedes and I connect.

Then the door opens and Letch deposits four women into the bus, slamming the door abruptly behind them. They smell like beer and cigarettes.

"Zom-B!" the girls shout in unison, a chorus that snaps Stan from his reverie.

You're calling my name but I gotta make it clear/I can't say baby where I'll be in a year.

Indeed.

Chapter 14:
Daytrippers, Part 2

"It's a freakin' zombie parade out there!"

"Did you see that zombie in the police uniform?"

"I thought they hated the sun..."

"I can't believe we're in a bus with DJ Zom-B!"

They won't stop. They're like "The View" on acid. Or some new MTV reality show on a horrific loop, just yammering, not a one of them even registering what the other is saying.

"Did you say there was one in a zombie uniform?" Ivan asks.

"Why can't you believe you're in here with DJ Zom-B?" asks Smack, sardonically.

"Whadda you mean parade?" asks Stan.

This gaggle of somewhat scantily clad women, having seemingly walked right off the set of a Russ Meyer movie, respond to Stan's soft, measured inquiry like he's blown a dog whistle and they are a pack of mongrels. Even while, again, his voice was considerably lower than both Ivan's and Smack's, never mind the fact that the music was still playing in the bus, albeit lower once Letch got back behind the wheel, his pain is somehow telepathic, each of the girls looking over to him.

"The police just loaded eight zombies into their paddy thingy," one gal informs him.

"Not eight, Lisa! It was, like, six. You always exaggerate."

"Six, eight..." she dismisses with a wave of her hand. "Who do we appreciate!?"

They high-five. Seriously. You can't make this shit up. Either they're high as fuck, or they could quite possibly be in shock.

"Are you girls serious?" Smack barks.

"Are you...handcuffed?" Lisa asks back. Another one of the girls laughs. Another high-five.

"Anywayyyyy," interjects a girl who hasn't said much yet. She may be the oldest of them all, her demeanor much more no-nonsense, though a Ritalin-chomping ten-year-old would be by comparison as well. She has a few grays curled up over her ears, a cowboy hat on, and her face has seen its share of sun. Still, her arms are jacked, bare in a wife-beater tee, wiry and bulging. She's attractive, tomboy chic. "I'm Janet." She extends her hands, and we shake. She can see that her squeeze causes me some pain and then releases it, genuinely sorry.

"I'm Luke," I tell her.

"Come on now! You're DJ Zom-B," Lisa corrects gregariously. How these two are together is beyond me; must be pure happenstance, as is the case in many a post-apocalyptic scenario—thrust together as they fled from a barnburner of some sort. Lisa's hair is blonder than can be humanly possibly, straight from a bottle and a few inches probably straight from wherever women buy hair extensions. Her boobs? Straight from a plastic surgeon's office. It's not as if all the work isn't worth every single penny, make no mistake: she's a knockout. But, thus far, cracking a book seems to have never dawned on her. Any egg, maybe, and definitely some windshields, but definitely not a book. "We won Tim McGraw tickets from you! Remember Jan?"

"Yeah, Lee." Okay, so Janet and Lisa actually are friends. "But, we've got more pressing matters." Lisa takes the chastisement well, opting to stare at her nails rather than question the pressing matters only Janet seems to grasp. Press-*on* nails. "So. Luke. The cops even outnumber the zombies out there. Why aren't they blowing all of these creatures to smithereens? Are they out of ammunition? Stun guns all they've got left?"

I look out the window and she's right. There's two more squad cars now, both full.

"You don't wanna know," Smack tells Janet, thankfully, as I don't have the faintest idea as to what to tell her. I would have probably gone with "I don't know" because the truth could turn this crew into a REAL *Girls Gone Wild*.

"I don't like guys telling me what I do or don't want," Janet informs Smack, her eyes suddenly like lasers on him. Gotta give him credit: he doesn't so much as shrug apologetically, and even tilts his head as if to convey to Janet that her independent woman routine is wasted on him, and particularly pointless right about now. "Why do you look so familiar anyway?"

The young lady sandwiched in between Janet and

Lisa, heretofore not introduced, stops tugging on the gum that she's been playing with, a strand almost a foot-long from lips to fingertips. "He's," she begins, but then has to get a good chew going on the cold, probably days old, gum again, "with her." She points at Mercedes, who has been curled up in the corner next to me, doing that thing that all girls do when they either want to conceal themselves or a blemish on their faces, something that usually only makes them that much more alluring: hiding conspicuously behind tangled jet black curls of hair. Janet, Lisa and the rest all turn to look at Mercedes. "She's the one who sings that song...ya know... *You use words like wild abandon, then don't text me back, you're so damn...*"

"*Random*!!" they all sing. 'Cept Janet.

"Mercedes?" Lisa seeks to clarify. "No way." Mercedes waves, comically even. From behind her mane, from the shadows of the corner.

"Can we get back to what I don't want to know?" Janet asks abruptly. "The police can't be out of ammo. We just left a prison, for Christ's sake. And where you made your broadcast—the one that landed us here—wasn't that a police station or some sort of federal building?" I nod yes. "Weapons there too, right?"

"Where did you hear him anyway?" inquires Ivan.

"Piece of crap TV at the bar we'd been holed up in for the past few days. Beginning to think we shoulda stayed there."

"You shoulda," Smack tells her.

"You're rude," Lisa fires back.

"I didn't mean it to be rude," Smack replies, sounding deadly serious, enough to silence this gaggle of hens. "You really, REALLY should have stayed there."

132

His words cast a pall on the bus, and everyone's eyes go everywhere else, most ending in the same place: Stan. He is trembling, remaining either a ticking bomb ready to explode or a bundle of nerves preparing to break down. He is the embodiment of all that we feel, all that is happening, has happened, and, likely, *will* continue to happen. That is, until nothing can anymore.

But one set of eyes, I notice peripherally, is not on Stan, but, rather, is focused solely on my hand, my right one, which I am rubbing profusely with my left. I am burying my thumb into my palm, a pressure point, and when I turn to meet Mercedes' eyes, she only smiles.

* * * * *

"Tell me what NIC stands for," I say to Ivan after a mile or so in silence, but his back is to me and he acts as if he doesn't hear me. "C'mon, I've done everything you've asked me to do, and we *are* in this mess together. Tell me!" He sits perfectly still, back seemingly "aimed" at me. I don't so much as kick him then but, moreover, *nudge* him with my right foot.

This is when I hear a formidable groan, and when Ivan turns to face me his eyes are rolling up, practically spinning in the sockets, unlike the zombies I've already encountered. They are practically reaching for the lids, looking to yank them like awnings.

"What the fu...!?" I manage, frantically pulling my legs back, and waking Mercedes in the process. Everyone on the bus has managed to doze off and here I've gone and wakened a zombie.

"Aaaarrrggghhh!!" Ivan releases, mightily, hands like

old trees in the winter, fingers the branches reaching for roof and window flying toward me.

I kick him in the face, and knock several of his teeth out of his mouth, one of them hitting Smack in the forehead, and the dubious DJ reacts like he has just been shot in the head by a BB gun.

Undeterred, Ivan continues at me, hands pawing, moans and groans a symphony of horror; I kick again but miss completely this time.

This is when his hands grab hold, when he manages to sink what's left of his teeth into me, even though they're decayed, brown as fallen leaves.

This is when he begins gnawing, my skin about as difficult to crack as that of a hotdog (which is to say not much), and he's in me, drinking my blood, spitting out veins like they're watermelon seeds.

This is when he begins purring, like my innards are akin to some exotic fish, delicate and rare, delicious and soothing to the soul, if zombies had souls.

This is when I wake up.

* * * * *

We are in front of the casino. My head is leaning against Mercedes' shin; not exactly on it but definitely up against it. I immediately scan the inside of the bus, beginning with Ivan. He looks like the same ol' Ivan. I try to assess just how much rotting might have taken place, if any, but, really, with him it's kinda hard to tell.

I scan the remainder of the bus. The girls are all asleep; I go from one to another and then another and on. But, Stan...he's still wide-awake, still trembling. And then there's Smack. Wide-awake, too, and staring right at me. He has reconciled with his discomfort, with the handcuffs, but leers in a way that suggests he does not like my turning said shin into a pillow.

"Bad dream, Pooky?" he asks mockingly.

"Yeah, actually," I reply honestly. "But what I'm waking up to ain't all that great, either."

"No shit. Any bright ideas?"

"Um, not really. Not yet anyway."

"Jesus, Zom-B. All that imagination, all that creativity...behind a microphone. Where is it now? You know why I'm handcuffed and you're not?"

"Do tell."

"Because you're not a threat to them."

"Or because I'm not stupid enough to show them that I'm one."

* * * * *

The helicopter sat in a makeshift landing. Makeshift in the sense that a helicopter has probably never been plopped down in it before, even while it is the very definition of expansive, vast and rural. Cows have stood here, grazed here, been tipped here, taken dumps here. Tractors have done pulls here, and taffy, too; a weathered sign reads "Durham Fairgrounds."

"Harrington," the radio crackled.

"Yep," he replied, like someone has snuck up on him, just talked off the ledge of a catnap. "Time to head back to Manhattan, sir?"

"That's a negative. We need you to do one more circle around the state."

135

"Dang, sir. Fellows got to head back."

"You're not Fellows. Are you questioning your assignment, son?"

"No, sir."

"We have to keep that state contained. All three states are almost completely shut down, and working on the fourth."

"This one already is shut down, sir. With all due respect. Not a living soul in sight for hours now. Not even one that isn't living. Like they're all together. Odd, really."

"Us still in contact is what's odd. One more time around, Harrington. That's an order. Out."

Frustrated, Harrington kicked open the door to his chopper and leapt out. He scanned the area and it is so wide open that to find a tree to pee behind he'd have to walk at least five minutes.

Zzzzzzziipppppp!

"Ahhhhh," he sighed, relieving himself on the burnt grass. He's too distracted by the sweet release to hear any of that brittle grass crack under the feet of three zombies, all of whom converge on his body, snapping his bones, one plunging his hand into Harrington's back and through his chest, grabbing a fistful of meat from off of his ribcage.

Chapter 15:
Undercard

When Letch "lets" us out of the bus he has his work cut out for him. A litany of questions come his way.

"What's going on here?"

"Why didn't you drive straight across state lines?"

"Why are we taking freakin' zombies with us!?"

"Where can I pee?"

They are all flying at him, hands with remarkably long fingernails spinning like propellers, no one more in his face than Janet. He is forced to step back, raise his rifle and aim.

"Wha...?" Janet manages. "What're you going to do—kill us? All of us?"

"If I don't," Letch begins coolly, "one o' them will."

We are surrounded by eight or so armed police officers.

"But...but..." stammers one of the girls who hasn't said much of anything yet that wasn't in unison with the others, "you're the law."

"Yep. In more ways than one, honey."

"Inside!" barks one of the other officers. "NOW!"

A chain gang without the chain, we all do as we are told, Letch's new recruits, while still launching questions like missiles, marching nonetheless. Smack, Ivan and I are side by side, all three with our eyes to the ground immediately before us, visions having begun to dance in my head of me gouging Letch's eyes out and tossing them into a zombie's awaiting mouth. My anger bubbles, years of yoga and therapy and chanting "Namiste" dissipating, with Stan directly behind me, a murdering spree or suicide waiting to happen. Or maybe just a lower-tier zombie having been created.

Once inside, we all share the awe of the spectacle that is a casino, particularly an abandoned one: the extraordinarily vaulted ceilings, endless array of art deco conversation pieces, and fountains where thousands of coins sit and bronzed literary figures with perched lips are poised to spit water. Alas, the water is not flowing, but the coins sit there, the cast away dreams of people long since gone, not a one of them having wished that the dead would never rise. That mighta helped.

Letch and his lackeys are confident enough that they have things under control that they huddle together somewhat, whispering to one another, not so much in a heated fashion, as if they're at odds, but there certainly is an element of divisiveness, or so it would appear, some heads shaking no and hands gesturing wildly.

"Seriously, what's going on?" Janet asks me, and really Ivan, too, who is standing beside me. "And don't give me some 'you don't wanna know' horror movie bullshit."

"Fact is we really don't know," Ivan tells her. "But, ignore their badges. They ain't the good guys."

Janet cranes her neck to focus on Smack, in my opinion suggesting to Ivan and I that Smack has just been elevated to a sort of leader status, someone to be looked to much more than either of us, our ignorance symbolic more so of defeat.

Smack can see the plea in her eyes, the white flag being offered. He sighs, wanting to tell her something, to give her a glimmer of hope, but there is only the truth, a truth he hasn't even been able to digest yet.

Still: "They have no intention of getting us out of Connecticut. Connecticut is being left for dead," says Smack.

"So we're just going to what? Hide here?"

"In a manner of speaking."

Nate is dispatched just then, off to fetch the zombies with a few other armed officers. We all begin to head for the arena, past roulette wheels and craps tables boasting a slight dusting, past buffets with food still sitting in some of the basins, mice skittering away upon hearing our grade-school, post-recess footsteps. Letch and his henchmen are completely on guard, employing a tactic obviously utilized when transferring ones to safety (even if they really aren't) while bracing for potential ambush. In this case, that would be another legion of undead emerging from, say, a ladies room or Bobby Flay burger joint.

"Remember when we saw Rascal Flatts here?" asks Lisa, still ridiculously oblivious to the increasingly dicey situation, as bubbly as champagne. Cheap champagne.

Nobody answers.

"I played here," Mercedes says softly.

"Opening for Christina Aguilera," points out Smack.

"Opening for that Nickelodeon girl with the hit TV show, who was opening for Christina Aguilera," Mercedes clarifies.

Smack grins charitably, her tireless ability to lessen her achievements clearly another of her characteristics that he is a sucker for; I find self-deprecation a high sign of high maintenance, even if I employ it on occasion myself.

We enter the arena. It is now gargantuan, like it could swallow Woodstock and still have room for dessert. But, that isn't the case; it's a relatively small venue, comparatively speaking.

I am reminded of Hospice, its endless floors, the nonstop cries, and the bedding being eternally swapped out, and the leaving your parents to watch *Wheel of Fortune* but having to turn it up considerably because the person next to them is writhing in agony and making no brittle bones about it. By morning his or her bed is empty, looking massive itself, as if the tiny, skin-and-bone figure in it the day before, who caused you so much misery—and it was compounded by the fact that you allowed it to, guilty never being selective—was decked out in a California King. Walking into the arena I feel the same bleak feeling I felt every day I walked into Hospice, which, all added together, is nine.

"Why did you do this?" Janet suddenly asks me. I turn to her and her big blue eyes look both vindictive and violated, like we grew up together and I just sent some sacred trust up in smoke, when instead I am simply a nameless, faceless, radio host; one who guided you through so many mornings and has just intentionally lured

140

you into some den of inequity, but still. "We trusted you. We came *because it was you.*"

"Has there been one second I haven't had a gun to my head since we met?" I say by way of answer. She gets it, turns to Letch and makes a run at him. He has no problem giving her the butt of his rifle, hard into her rib cage. Her cowboy hat flies off and a mane of streaked brown hair is released, covering her face as she hits the floor.

"Now, now," he says. "Knew you were feisty. Your match is gonna be the undercard to watch!"

Her girlfriends are by her side, gently helping her to her feet. "What do you mean match?" one asks. After all, who in their right mind—or even outta their mind—could deduce that the police would corral what few humans were left in a given state during a zombie uprising and rather than, I dunno, protect and serve them, would serve them UP to said zombies in fights to the death? You'd need one hell of an imagination.

Just as Letch enthusiastically declares Janet's undercard "the one to watch" the zombies begin to file in, the sounds of stun guns and tasers like a mosquitoes getting zapped by one of those lamps on a front porch in summer: constant. Janet's match just might be up.

"Letch!" shouts one of the officers. "We gotta get Reardon in there! I swear I still see his drunken Irish eyes in that head!" He's pointing to a zombie in a tattered police uniform, which the girls had mentioned upon being led into the bus. Reardon obviously didn't fare too well in a previous altercation with a zombie and has now become one. All code out the window, his brethren are fully prepared to see how he'll do up against an armed human, rather than put him out of his misery, soldier/Viking/pirate

141

mentality be damned. Okay, maybe not pirate, but I'm pretty sure about those other ones.

"Hah!" laughs Letch. "I was actually looking to get a steel cage female match out of the way but, sure, bring Reardon over. Our li'l pal Smack here is itchin' to take out some of his private school hostility on a cop. Even if it is a zombie cop."

"Private school? I went to public school in the Bronx," Smack corrects.

"Yo," adds Letch, to an indignant Smack. "Went to public school in the Bronx, *yo*. Isn't that it?"

"Whatever, man. You guys are an Ice-T record come to life. You're making everything he sang about the law right on the money."

"And now he makes money *playing* the law, doesn't he?" one officer astutely points out. Check-fucking-mate. "For years now. Every acting job he's a cop."

"Well, I'm not fighting."

"Then you're dying."

"Then I'm dying."

"Smack!" shrieks Mercedes, and I do mean shrieks. All of her anxiety medication has definitely worn off.

"I'll fight him." The words come from far behind us all, and they are low yet foreboding.

It's Stan.

He is standing, hands on his hips like George Reeves in a promo shot for the old "Superman" TV series. The final season. Shoulders broad, yes, and hands like cinder blocks, sure; however, also, doughy as he is angry, and as gray as he is brooding. Stan cannot possibly think he stands a chance and, what's more, I don't think he wants one.

"Wow. Ya know, that actually could be interesting," Letch ponders aloud. "No fuel like loss."

"No, no, I changed my mind. I'll do it," Smack interjects.

Letch shoots him a look, and then promptly shoots him down. "Either you're gonna make a break for me and get shot, which will be anti-climactic, or you'll go out a hero, which would also be anti-climactic. I'm liking the Stan/Reardon undercard more and more."

"What's an undercard?" inquires Lisa.

"Shuddup Lee," a still-wincing Janet warns.

"Zap ol' Reardo over here," Letch commands. The uniformed zombie is prodded over not unlike a cow or some other farm animal, alternately corralled and agitated. Before we know it the undead is being kicked into Stan's direction and it's on.

Stan charges him like a bull and topples Reardon. Letch and his cronies cheer: "Oooohhhh!!"

Then a sound, like a tomato being smashed onto pavement. A fountain of blood rises, high and then even higher. The zombie ate Stan's Adam's apple as if that's exactly what it was, an apple. He dies immediately. It proceeds to gorge on the remnants of Stan's throat, plucking both Stan's arms off at the same time.

One of the girls faints and on her way down whacks her head against the railing around one of the VIP boxes. Sprawled out on the floor of the arena her body begins to convulse. Again, the chorus of depraved officers: "Ohhhhh!!!"

The girls gather around her. "Chelsea!" one shouts. "Will one of you help her!? What kind of animals are you!?"

"Is that rhetorical?" Ivan asks, approaching Chelsea, who is presently in the midst of one hell of a spasm. Her torso then rises into the air like an exorcism is being performed, and she suddenly goes limp. Ivan presses to fingers to her neck and what he says next comes as a shock to exactly no one, except her bar-hopping gal pals. "She's gone."

"Gone?" Janet asks incredulously. "GONE!?" She turns towards Letch, towards all of them, a girl figuratively and literally gone wild. "You sick motherfuckers!!" She makes a beeline in their direction; a wobbly one—probably sporting a broken rib or two from the butt of the shotgun—but a beeline nonetheless.

Nate sends a female zombie in her direction, zapping the female zombie directly next to that one out of commission. My knee-jerk reaction is actually to help, to join in the fray, but, honestly, from my vantage point the whole fucking thing is Orwellian. I can't suss out the difference between the civilized and the undead. It's the last chapter of "Animal Farm" in a manner of speaking.

Janet lands a kick in the zombie's chest, and thanks to the cowboy boot and accompanying spur, it sends the monstrosity back several feet and also causes it to emit a yelp. Then it's a back kick from Janet, Tae-Bo Tuesday and Thursday nights for a few years there, maybe even an elective in college or the result of a restraining ordered ex-boyfriend; this one sees to it that said spur opens the zombie's neck.

"See?" Letch shouts exuberantly. "Knew that one was going to give us a hell of a match!"

But the aberration still clamors for cartilage and its condiments. Undeterred, it reaches and this time Janet goes with a right hook, which lands firmly in the freshly opened throat. The zombie grabs hold of Janet's arm and pulls her toward her.

"Stop it! It's going to kill her! She'll die, too! Please save her!" pleads Lisa. The pleas fall on deaf ears, of course. Well, deaf uniformed ears anyway.

Smack leaps into action, hands cuffed behind his back not all that much of a hindrance in the heat of battle, even if it's someone else's. He jumps up onto the railing of the VIP box and then back-flips off, in a way that gets the zombie into a strangle hold. They are back to back, but for a nanosecond, and then with a jarring tug to the left he breaks the creature's neck.

There is not a jaw in the house that isn't dropped, and I mean that literally; the flies the dead have amassed are zeroing in on these mouths, torpedoing toward them, only to be swatted away by all of us.

There is also not a weapon in the arena not aimed at every single one of us, two less than two inches from Smack's face. The sounds of weapons being cocked, ready to fire, silence the mini-melee. All right, maybe not mini, but it could have gone on now, couldn't it have, could have continued to an even grislier conclusion.

"Impressive for a guy who makes funny sounds on records for a living," Letch commends Smack. "You just nominated yourself for the ultimate steel cage match with our boy Reardon in a li'l bit. Now how d'ya feel?"

"Outside of the dislocated shoulder?" Smack says by way of reply.

Have I mentioned that Mercedes has glued herself to him, face pressed to his sweaty, heaving chest, a veritable comic book cover come to life? And who can blame her?

If there is anyone who can save us all, it's him; jury's still out on if we all *should* be saved anyway. I'm kinda rooting for the zombies, not that I say as much. Truth is, this all has been enlightening in a way: my anger couldn't ever really go anywhere as long as people didn't; I hate people, have been let down by too many, and unimpressed by even more. What a revelation.

"Nate, un-cuff Mr. Pay-per-View so he can pop that shoulder back in. Meantime, while we wait to see if we get any more company, let's all get the freaks into one place," Letch instructs, " and the zombies into another."

Chapter 16:
Meat 'n Greet

How and/or why I wind up alone with Mercedes is anyone's guess. Maybe because we're the "talent." We sit in a tiny room behind the stage in the arena practically awaiting instructions, not unlike actual appearances; ya know, a meet-n-greet with the folks running the whole shebang where they tell me how I'm to address the crowd, who our sponsor is, and then how to introduce on Mercedes. Surreal continues to be an understatement.

Minutes after being locked in here, there was a knock. One of the officers brought in a couple in their 20's who were filthy, clothes torn but otherwise pretty together. The officer couldn't be more than 25 and seemed in stark contrast to his contemporaries. Acne-scarred and anxious, he made introductions, while all the while he avoided eye contact with me and sweat profusely. When he did make eye contact with Mercedes genuine sorrow and confusion had clearly confiscated his corneas.

"It's really you," the male half of the couple said,

147

awestruck when he should have been dumbstruck, by now anyway. "We were heading to Monhegan Island, but..."

He trailed off, thankfully, lest the guilt become too overbearing for both Mercedes and I. The female in his company asked Mercedes for an autograph. She obliged and then they were whisked away.

"I can't believe all this," Mercedes says. "This is where I'm going to die." She begins to sob, her fragility never more apparent, even while mine is only nonexistent due to my being an idiot. An idiot whose lifelong anger would be ideal right about now, but has grown accustomed to only showing up when I wish it wouldn't.

Her face, makeup all washed away, and her tiny frame, contorted, more so as the sobs increase, reveal yet again just how young she is, catapulted into the showbiz world something she wore well, but it came with a price. She paid it, stood tall, taking the stamp on the back of her hand; but this subsequent turn of events is now bombarding somebody who was stripped of all self-esteem, of all the confidence she lay in the hands of suits and ties and "yes" guys. The yes turned to no, and the business being show, she is prepared for nothing, like so many before her, let alone the something being a zombie uprising.

"You're not going to die here," I tell her, and I manage to sound convincing. I have no plan, but the words roll off my tongue in a way that suggests that I do. Why I really feel this way is Smack, and I say as much. "Smack would never let that happen."

"Smack is going to die right in front of us, in just a little while! Even if he...if he...wins, that dirt-bag cop will just make him fight again. He can't KEEP winning!"

"He loves you, you know," comes next, and I'm not sure why. Maybe because I have always been in awe of love, the wound from my one fall still so Goddamned fresh, unstitched and infected, even if it was a silly three-week-long lifetime ago. So, I think that this will come as some consolation, despite the fact that I know she's aware of his feelings already. Death's hand is easier to shake if somebody loved you at some point, if in your life you were deemed lovable by someone other than your mother or father, but its grip is even more crushing to someone whose heart never swelled, whose love was never returned. What a life to let go of. That's my two cents anyway.

"Smack doesn't love me," Mercedes says back, like a mad woman, tears and frustration fusing the declaration; she is adamant, but not indignant. "We're music partners. Feelings...happen...when you make art together. What does that matter now anyway!?" I can't argue, just let her wail. "We played here together, Smack and I. I remember it like it was yesterday. Hah! A thousand yesterdays ago."

"More like a hundred," I correct. "I remember it, too. You killed it that night. Is that inappropriate?"

Mercedes laughs, a glorious, proof-of-Heaven laugh, one that spits in the face of the situation and gets heartier upon seeing my facial expression, a curled up, intentionally goofy look on my face.

"And you did some stupid sketch on your radio show the next day about me having thrown a tizzy fit because there were no yellow M&M's in my dressing room. Your imitation of me was horrible."

We actually smile about it. "Who cares about the stupid bits I did on my radio show? Why did they ever

149

even bother you? Everyone does them. Perez Hilton said you were dressed like a 'color blind hooker who just stepped on a rake' the next night at your Madison Square Garden show!" I even do the quotation marks with my fingers as I regurgitate the Hilton quip. "That's verbatim. I remember."

"Yours bothered me more."

"I know. Why?"

"My brother showed me some clips of your band Gangland on YouTube."

"It was Gangbusters, but anyway..."

"Gangbusters, sorry. But, really? Ooph. Corny."

"You were saying?"

"You're a musician. Shit, you can play. Potshots from other artists...they hurt more than just some talking puppet or writer for a website."

"Hm. Thanks. I guess. And I guess that makes sense, too." After a lengthy pause. "I'm sorry."

"So, why did you stop playing? Please don't do some 'the record industry is shit rant,' either."

"Well, it is, but that isn't the reason. The real reason is, I broke my hand. By punching a wall. Decidedly unglamorous."

"A wall-puncher, huh? I wouldn't have guessed that."

With the pharmaceutical cobwebs cleared away, Mercedes seems like an entirely different person, clever and funny and feet more squarely on the ground than I had already discovered and told Ivan, even if she just recently got her sea-legs back. She's looking at me studiously, trying to "see" me for the first time. I guess I'm doing the same.

"Punching walls is really fucking stupid," she finally

says. "That's 'boy in high school who becomes a sociopath' territory."

"Ah," I dismiss with a wave of my hand, laughing just the same. "I was doing it then, too."

"Do you still? Now would be a great time."

"Nam-myoho-renge-kyo."

"No shit? Chanting!?" Mercedes is downright giddy. Her eyes are alight and I'd be lying if I didn't say they were like a jolt of energy. Her laugh's infectious, her curiosity contagious; in her presence my anger—a constant my entire life—could never resurface. "Buddhism keeps you from punching walls?"

"My broken hand is what keeps me from punching walls," I confide. She is inches from my face, and I can feel her breath. I want to steal a kiss but am not a "kiss stealer." That first time that I was in love, those supposed glory days of high school, my heart was stomped on by a girl whose kisses transported me but who was also generous with them: my friends, my enemies, a guidance counselor. And when I'd ask about these kisses I'd hear about, my eyes wide and liquid, a willingness to believe any lie told to me, it was always the same reply: he stole a kiss. They were always stolen. Can a kiss truly be? Borrowed, maybe, but not stolen. There has to be compliance.

Here, though, and now...I want one in the face of this craziness, because of it, and from Mercedes to boot because it seems like there would be something healing in it. Her eyes are fixed on mine, and the distance between us is even less than a second ago when my mind first began to wander.

"Lovebirds!"

It's Letch. *His* eyes are more maniacal than ever, and another officer is behind him, with a female zombie in tow; it is shackled, with a ball in its mouth. He startles both Mercedes and I and whatever was about to just happen—or not happen—goes where all such moments go, into the ether and promptly filed under "?"

"It's almost show-time. Let's be professional here." He leans over, grabs Mercedes' face, which galvanizes me. He manages to add, "Besides, what would Smack..." But, I land a hard blow against the side of his face before he truly finishes the sentence. He stumbles onto his side while his sidekick quickly tasers me. It's incredible, the painful rush of electricity through my body, the way it makes me immediately cognizant of all my nerve endings and how my insides feel like one big brush fire. I am spastic on the floor, and my zapping makes the zombie go wild, even while restrained. She's making supremely inhuman sounds, as opposed to "formerly human."

Letch grabs me by my shirt and lifts me up toward him. He honestly doesn't seem all that bothered by the punch. "You're the last one I expected to play hero," he says in a whisper, so much so I don't even think Mercedes can hear it. His breath is atrocious, the zombie's decayed flesh preferable. He drops me back down and I whack the back of my head on the floor. Mercedes is quick to take me into her arms, resting my head in her lap.

"You're lucky I ain't taking her with me right now!" shouts Letch, pointing at Mercedes. "Instead of this freak."

They leave just then, the zombie being the one I feel the most compassion for of the trio.

"What did he mean by that?" Mercedes wants to

know. What do I say? It was a rape reference? He's off to bang that zombie against her...its...will?

I say nothing, especially since there is something I want to know myself. Was that a withered, rotted tattoo of a crucifix on the zombie's bare arm?

* * * * *

The first time I attended an anger management meeting I thought I had stumbled into Alcoholics Anonymous by mistake.

My meeting was taking place in an indistinguishable building downtown, the type where the entire bottom floor is dedicated to the messed up, mixed up, and making up: AA to the left, Anger Management to the right, Conflict Resolution down the hall, Self-Esteem & Meditation across from that, Personal Growth by the restrooms. (That way, when ya had to pee or take a dump you got to hear someone repeating "I can do it," which, admittedly, sometimes helped with stage-fright and/or a stubborn bowel movement.)

Each room was dank, dusty, and unkempt, with either cracked windows or ones sealed shut. Everyone sat in a circle, with the mediator ever the anchor, and always obvious due to placement, never mind demeanor, dress, and clipboard. Without signs taped up to the door that said which class it was you'd never be able to tell the difference until you were knee-deep into someone's sob story. The faces are equally blank, save for the Personal Growth, who are in a constant striving mode, ever the little engine that could and will, but the striving factor often translated to their faces looking pained with constipation, which, really, could still be considered blank.

Some of the rooms were alarmingly quiet, maybe one person speaking and doing so after much prodding and scripted encouragement, which usually meant the monologue was delivered through gritted teeth, loaded with pregnant pauses, and devoid of emotion, sans embarrassment.

I refused to speak—or, "share"—the first three times out. Then finally I cracked. The mediator just kept saying, "Luke..." and "Anything..." She even dragged my then-former line of work into the equation, playfully inquiring if I might be more comfortable with a microphone.

I hated her face. I hated everyone's face in that room. And that's really all I said: "I just...hate people."

The guy sitting next to me didn't even seem to register the comment, his infuriatingly dumbfounded expression still intact, mouth open the exact same amount it was week after week, same bubble aching to form on his cracked lips. He was in a stupor. I remember exactly what I thought of him, what I told my mother he looked like, this one lone character who truly prevented me from embracing the class and its idiotic exercises: A zombie.

Chapter 17:
Main Event

As Mercedes and I are led up the ramp towards the arena it is not thunderous applause, or a boisterous audience whose constant chatter alerts to a pending performance that greets us; it is instead a deadly silence, save for a few rows of people who are clearly trying to piece together just what the hell they've somehow managed to safely travel many miles to.

I kinda feel responsible. I say as much to Ivan who is, well, jerry-rigging what equipment is there to see if we can get any sound whatsoever. Some electricity could still be had, and generators could still get kicked on, never mind anything relying on batteries or a satellite feed.

"Ya kinda are, kid," he tells me. "It's your broadcast they're responding to." Ivan—the man whose transformation into a zombie has to be the longest in documented history—pulls no punches, even while said broadcast couldn't have even taken place without his help. But, damned if he'll split the blame. "You're the one who

155

wanted to go on the air in the first place."

He's got me there. "Some of these people, though...where are they from? We met a couple and I swear they sounded like they were from Maine. One of them said something about Monhegan Island. Isn't that a few miles off its coast?"

Ivan looks up at me, smiles. His teeth have been colored in by the tobacco industry, and he's got nostril hairs that could slice bread. "Remember that N.I.C. you asked me about?" I nod yes. "'National Information Center.' That last playback went national. The whole fucking country heard it."

"Then you're the reason they're here!" I spout, not focused on what he's really saying.

"Christ, kid, if that's how ya wanna look at it. But why not look at the bigger picture? Your broadcast came up on radio, TV, scrolls—shit, lottery machines—*across the country*. The big guns are coming."

"Yeah, but are they gonna be aimed at us?"

"At least at first," Ivan says coolly. Then he thumps his forefinger against the head of the microphone and it can be heard across the arena, lightly but still heard. We've got sound.

Letch emerges from the ramp directly across from the one we just took, which means he went halfway around the entire venue just for privacy and who knows what else. He is utterly dramatic, entering like a gladiator, albeit one who won't be doing battle. That being the case, he is more the king, the one who need be entertained. He strides into the center of the arena floor and ostentatiously places a box on the floor. Then he leaves it there, guarded by a police lackey and joins me on the stage, taking the

156

microphone into his hand.

"Good evening, ladies and gentlemen," he says, more matter-of-factly than theatrically. "Standin' next to me is your host for the evening. Some of you may recognize his voice. Maybe even his face, from a bird-shit target of a billboard ten years ago or so. He's been on the radio in these parts for years. DJ Zom-B!" Not one single clap, and Letch is promptly appalled. "I...um...realize his radio name ain't all that enticing right about now, folks. But show some respect. I said...this is YOUR HOST!" The claps, the applause, comes...scattered, befuddled and, as such, lackluster. Not that I mind, of course. "You also may recognize this little lady, pop star Mercedes!" The applause actually doubles, even some whistles. The celebrity can still garner awe, in the most heinous of situations. I think that knowledge, that ever-increasing fact, played a major role in my simmering hatred of the human race. Mercedes hangs her head, stares at her feet. "But make no mistake. They are NOT your entertainment. YOU are."

With that Letch signals the guard by the box, who then lifts the top off and kicks it over. A zombie's head comes tumbling out. The zombie he was just...with.

* * * * *

Letch and his cronies had it down to a science now. Taser them into as much of a submission as you can taser a zombie into. Cuff their hands and legs and gag them. The first rape had come as the direct result of rage, of one officer having successfully subdued one, and as the adrenaline pumped and he realized he could kill it at his leisure he sought to humiliate it, which you can't truly do to something like a zombie, but the process—the removal of clothes, the slapping of the face, and then the backside; it entertained Letch, who was looking on, and the cop just sort of went with it, neither of them saying anything during, or even after. It was an unspoken one-time thing. But the hours stretched out, turned into a day or two, the zombies were everywhere, the government had disowned them.

When they did finally speak of it, the officer had conveyed the sensation thusly: "It's conquest, this sorta humans triumphing thing, ya know? Plus it actually feels good." Letch was in.

When Letch's latest sidekick confined his latest victim in a tiny green room in the basement of the venue, it was rape plain and simple. But now the rape was no longer enough. Such is the slippery slope of doing bad things. You keep raising the bar, lowering your standards. Breaking its neck immediately after release provided more pleasure than the release.

It took Letch and his underling twenty minutes to cut the head off.

Early in his career, Andrew Letchcow had taken a bullet in the leg for a young black girl at a hillbilly bar where some rednecks pulled out handguns and began hurling racial epithets; he talked a mental patient off a ledge; he took part in dozens of foot chases, most of which ended in arrests; he talked a father in the middle of an ugly divorce into admitting that he had his daughter stashed at a friend's house after two days of feigning dismay at her "disappearance" to anyone who would listen, let alone film him.

By the end of his career, barely any of the blow was making it back to the precinct house, the hookers were cutting him in and giving him freebies, and his arrests were usually guys who mouthed off at his inappropriate flashing of his badge and other antics at local bars.

It was a slow descent, one barely registered by his coworkers, superiors, or even Andrew himself. But when the thought came to break the zombie's neck—not the rape, the insaneness of intercourse with the undead, but the violence afterwards—he knew he turned a corner there. Midway through the head removal he was sitting comfortably in madness.

* * * * *

The gasps sound staged. *Seeing* zombies appears to be one thing, but one of their heads rolling out of a box is seemingly another altogether. Maine is stunned.

"Your government has abandoned you. Left you for dead. Left you WITH the dead. Tonight...we show 'em who's boss!" The police cheer wildly.

One of them leads a sopping wet zombie out into the center of the arena. None of us had really smelled the gasoline until just now, so preoccupied we were by what was going on around us, and the fumes stifled so by the stale air, the rotting flesh, the rodent excrement, and our own unbathed body odors. He takes the cuffs off, both hands and feet, and allows it to meander about for a few moments, for its hunger to fuel more rage, excuse the pun.

Then he lifts a lighter up to wild applause. Flicks it, flame up like the middle finger. He bends down, ignites some of the gasoline on the floor and it races towards the zombie's body. It goes up in flames. Its howls are guttural, decidedly different than the sounds they make either feeding or being fed a blade. The applause grows exponentially, and Mercedes tugs on my arm. I expect to turn and see the panic in her eyes having reached a new high, but instead she is pointing over to the Maine folks. A few of them—not all, but a few—are cheering along with the police.

* * * * *

Letch hands the microphone over to me, without turning his head. Instead he gives another nod, to two more officers, a carefully choreographed production being unveiled. One brings Smack out, and the other this Reardon, a former law enforcer. "Introduce the match," he commands.

I glance at Mercedes, at a complete loss as to what to do next, what to say—if anything at all. Part of me just wants to leap on Letch from behind and snap *his* neck. There is an anger I can tap into, and recruit my violence; a different anger than my normal, but an anger nonetheless.

But, what good would it truly do? I'd be shot on sight. There really seems to be no way out of this. Furthermore, with regard to Mercedes, is he actually going to have her sing at some point? Some bizarre halftime concert, wherein she either does one of her songs acapella or to some beats he'll hand over to Ivan?

Speaking of Ivan, I look over at him and he's in total engineer mode. He's lost all will to live, or moreover, to stop this madness. Is this merely a byproduct of his outrageously, even infuriatingly slow transformation, or am I merely the slowest to surrender?

"Do it!" Letch commands, startling me. My body twitches as he snaps me out of my reverie, which amuses him. He laughs a pitiful laugh.

"Okay...uh...so Simon Bar Sinister over here has decreed that there shall be death matches. Or undead matches, really. First up, for the living, Smack." I hear myself gulp, almost having an out of body experience, looking down at myself, at me making this announcement, the surreal nature of it all ballooning to heretofore unseen proportions. "For the dead, a cop named Reardon. A deejay against a zombie cop!"

Letch likes that last part. Mercedes rushes to my side, very B-movie, very Raquel Welch. "What're we gonna do?" she asks, clinging to me, as I stare out at the madness, a glint in my eye, a movie poster at the ready.

Out in the middle of the arena, Smack is let loose, handcuffs doffed. The cop holding him kicks him forward and holds up his nightstick. "Letch wants this to be interesting. No knife." He tosses Smack the stick. It lands in front of him and bounces. His arms have been handcuffed behind his back for so long, his shoulder recently dislocated, he cannot help but to stretch them, rub them, get the nerve endings going again.

"What? A fucking nightstick? Why not just kill me?"

Reardon is let loose and "aimed" at Smack.

"Use it or lose it," the cop tells Smack.

Smack begins to back towards the seating area, but strategically placed police, with weapons drawn, force him to engage. He rushes the zombie and smacks it in the head and it just...goes down. Letch and his cronies go wild. Then Letch looks at me quizzically. So I look back

161

at him the exact same way.

"Play by play!" he shouts.

"Oh, come on!" I blast right back at him, aghast at the preposterousness. He spits onto the floor by way of response. "Play-by-play wasn't in my contract." I murmur, under my breath, to Mercedes. This one doesn't make her laugh. "And he's down!" I shout, as hammy as can be. "Or should I say it's down? Point, human!"

Now it's Smack's turn to shoot the befuddled look. He can't believe I'm going along with this, but isn't he doing the same? Perhaps driven by my ludicrous emceeing, adding to an already-pumping adrenaline, he stomps over, mounts the zombie and simply snaps his neck. It would be the epitome of anticlimactic if the entire crowd didn't go nuts, especially some of the gang from Maine, those of whom surely haven't figured out yet that their turn to brawl is in the Playbill.

So I go continue with even more zeal. "Whoa! Will you look at that? Smack has killed...*the already dead*. Hey! What if there's a zombie cat somewhere around here? He's on, like, his tenth life and probably thinking, 'Are you kidding me? Nine wasn't enough?'" I actually get some laughs. This is bizarre Byzantine bullshit, but it's happening.

Letch raises his hand to one of his guys. At first I think he's shooting him the peace sign, but it's in actuality him requesting two more zombies. They are prodded in Smack's direction, about to have their cuffs snapped off.

"You're not serious?" exclaims Smack. "How long is this gonna go on for?"

Letch replies, "'Til you lose."

The zombies stumble toward Smack. He hits one in

the face with the nightstick, and the other in the stomach as he's coming off the first hit, and follows it with an uppercut.

"The humans are a force to be reckoned with!" I shout, to feverish cheers. No boos. But, then again, zombies don't boo.

As if irked by my declaration anyway, one of the zombies gets hold of Smack and basically serves him up to his zombie brother. As that zombie opens wide, and I hear Mercedes scream, I drop the microphone. But, Smack pulls a fast one, and spins the zombie holding him out to front and center where his zombie sidekick bites *him* instead.

"Let's go!" Letch barks, and I initially think he's rooting for the zombies, which, to be honest, he probably is. Instead, he is barking at me, to pick up the mike. "Pick it up."

"No more," I say. "This is madness. Mad Max outtakes."

He aims his gun at Mercedes. I look down and see the zombie head just a few feet away, the rest of her, including the arm with the crucifix tattoo, probably left on the floor of the room she was last in. Could it be the woman who's haunted my dreams for so long? A mom whose death I allowed to happen by not speaking up? Whose...well...second death I allowed the exact same way?

I step in front of Mercedes, defy Letch. Feel that old familiar feeling: hate. It courses through my veins, not unlike shooting heroin, I'm sure. Hate makes me feel invincible, driven by mindless superiority and disregard for my own life. *Kill me first, motherfucker. Kill me first. I*

163

can literally hear his finger on the trigger, zero perspiration no doubt, his heartbeat probably not even accelerated—more so by the bout, if anything. But, I don't so much as flinch. Not only am I certain he won't shoot, but I wouldn't give him the satisfaction of seeing me cower even if I thought otherwise.

That's when he shoots me.

* * * * *

I'm only out for a minute, maybe two. The first voice I hear is Mercedes, soothing, nurturing, genuinely concerned. There's also a smidge of damsel in distress gratitude thrown in there. "Are you okay? Please be okay! I can't believe you took a bullet for me!"

Then I hear Ivan, and he's the first I see as well. He's pressing on the area beneath the bullet-hole, ostensibly to stop the bleeding, though I don't realize that straightaway. Instead, I just see him leaning onto my wound and groaning, blood everywhere.

"Don't eat me!" I scream at him, shoving him away. I almost go black again, grasping at my bloodied shoulder, writhing in agony. Mercedes continues to rock me gently, despite my sudden jerking. "Don't let him eat me," I plead. "He's turning into one of them!"

Ivan looks as perplexed as Mercedes. "He must be in shock," he tells her.

"Bullshit!" I snap. "Show her your arm!"

Called out, Ivan can only roll up his sleeve. His cheeks get flush red, but he shows the bite-mark to Mercedes, which doesn't much look like a bite-mark anymore, if it ever even did.

"What...happened?" Mercedes asks sweetly, reaching to touch it.

"Don't touch it!" I exclaim, grabbing her hand. More pain for me. "He was bitten by one of them!"

"Is that what you thought all this time, kid? I did this myself, day one of all this shit. My original thinkin' was I'd rather off myself than give them the pleasure, I'm sorry to say. Fuckin' coward." He looks at Mercedes. "Oops. Sorry."

"It's cool."

"You mean you're not...changing? Becoming one of them? And all this time I was watching my back...?" I manage.

"That was you watching your back? You slept pretty soundly for a guy bunking with a zombie-to-be."

The black is coming again, everything going blurry. Out in the center of the arena it sounds like a free-for-all, perpetual chaos. I wonder if Smack is still among the living. But, the lights are going, going...

And the familiar sound of a trigger being clicked into place brings me around. "Well, if you ain't gonna be one of them," begins Letch, "then you're gonna fight one of them."

Ivan rises to his feet, covered in my blood. There's so much. I've got to be dying. Mercedes' eyes are working overtime, on me, then on Ivan, then out to where Smack must still be doing his thing. Some of the cops are even still cheering, two different stages going at once, not unlike Lollapalooza. Zombie-palooza.

"I'll fight," Ivan says. "YOU."

"How old West," Letch replies. "Might even take you up on it if you weren't a puss who tried to kill himself a few days ago. I liked you better when I thought a zombie took a bite outta you. Had more respect for you. Deputy...? Bring our suicidal human here down to center stage." Nothing. "Nate! Where the fuck is that asshole anyway?"

Ivan and Letch are staring each other directly in the eye, ever the standoff. "Looks like you're gonna have to bring me down yourself. If you can."

Letch relies on his steel yet again, pointing it more squarely, a coward of another variety, the even worse kind; not that I think Ivan a coward at all really—just a guy having a knee-jerk reaction to the streets he'd walked for years suddenly being flooded with the undead. "Oh, I can. If you're wounded—already bleeding—that'll be even more entertaining to watch. These things smell that, like you and I smell garlic."

Suddenly, a tiny red light, a laser, lands directly on Letch's nose. I follow Ivan's eyes following it like it's an insect. "Nobody move!" is heard through a bullhorn.

We're surrounded by FBI.

Not being ones for heeding such orders or, rather, comprehending them, the zombies continue in their incessant march for blood and guts. This being the case, a barrage of gunfire results, the precision and amount of time in which it is all unleashed stupefying; zombies simply drop like rain, a summer squall, quick, hard, and then it's over. In less than a minute, a huffing and puffing, chest-heaving Smack is standing in the center of a circle of fallen zombies.

I am promptly helped to my feet by Mercedes despite the FBI's command and subsequent Bay of Pigs recreation. Not in a petulant or even hasty manner, but moreover because the cavalry has arrived, plus I feel as if I've done enough lying down. The FBI slowly converge on us all and, for whatever reason—more than likely simply being out of his mind—Letch makes a run for it. The FBI don't seem to know what to make of it so while another "don't move" is announced, this time sans bullhorn, they do not fire so much as one round in his direction.

So, I do the only thing I can think of doing: I chase after Letch, flesh wound and all.

* * * * *

As the FBI swooped in, Janet, Lisa and the girls wasted no time in suggesting they keep their weapons drawn and aimed at the police.

"Are you all right?" one agent asked straightaway.

"Don't let them get away!" Janet shouted.

"No zombies are getting away tonight, ma'am. They're all dead. Here at the casino anyway."

"Not the zombies—them!" She pointed at the police.

"I don't understand."

"Were your eyes open as you burst in here? The cops were standing around as that guy fought zombies! They were making him fight them! They've all lost it, everyone with a badge." The rookie, head hung low, shame making his stomach churn, lifted his weapon, aimed it at his head, took his life.

* * * * *

I chase Letch down the hallway, towards the

restrooms, green rooms, VIP rooms. It isn't easy for me, and I can see my shadow does not look all that different from a zombie's. I am moving like a veritable Frankenstein's monster, thanks to the gunshot wound just inflicted on me. By the guy I'm chasing, which helps in my pursuit, a back-up generator of sorts. But, my shadow distracts me. It is then met by a similar-looking shadow.

"Nate!" barks Letch. "Finally! Where ya been, boy? Will you finish off this motherfucker while I start up a squad car and get us the hell outta here?"

Letch may or may not be planning on bringing Nate along. I honestly think it's all a matter if Nate can make it to the car in time. In other words, *kill me in time.*

Letch pushes the door open and light floods into the cavernous hallway. There are maybe a half dozen helicopters out there. As the light rushes in, stretching my shadow and Nate's as well, I see one beam crawl across Nate's face. It is blank, bloodless and gaunt. He's crossed over. A zombie.

Alas, Letch only discovers this when he turns back towards him, mid-sentence. "Shit! We're cornered like rats. Get in front of me, Na..."

But, Nate is on him, a rat on cheese. Letch's plan to turn him into a human shield backfires, as Nate is busy with plans of his own.

"Enjoy your meal," I say, turning quickly and heading back up to the arena.

Letch's screams remind me of Axl Rose's vocals on *Welcome to the Jungle.* Or is it *Sweet Child o' Mine*?

* * * * *

"It was like the lion's den, ya know?" Lisa told an agent taking a statement. "Scandinavia?

"Huh?" the agent burped.

Meanwhile, Smack rested, for the first time since this all went down, legs crossed, alone. Mercedes looked on for a minute or so, debated approaching him, maybe seeing him for the first time, maybe letting herself. Maybe, maybe, maybe.

"Was that really you out there?" she finally asked, from a distance, always a distance—the one she had kept all these years, admittedly, a different one than this one. "I didn't know you had that in you."

"You don't really know me," he replied, looking away.

"No," conceded. "I guess not."

Epilogue

As the FBI has their fair share of secretive exchanges, which one would think would make all of us uneasy yet doesn't, Janet and I actually share a fairly touching goodbye. We've been given helicopter assignments and will not be traveling together. Why we all cannot decide this ourselves, too, should be cause for concern, but one cannot help but think the worst is behind he or she after the kinda thing that just happened, really happened.

"You stood right in front of her," Janet says, no trace of tomboy. "Where I come from they call that chivalry." She tips her cowboy hat toward me, and then gently flicks my chin.

"Yeah? Where do you come from?"

"Milford, Connecticut."

"Janet, we're in that one," Lisa interjects, pointing over to a beauty of a chopper, propeller spinning full throttle. "DJ Zom-B! Are you coming with us?" I nod my head no. Smack, Ivan, and I are probably all going straight to the hospital. "Well, bye-ee!"

Lisa gives me a huge hug, her disinterest in segue

jarring. Her friends all line up for hugs as well. They're killing my shoulder, haphazardly bandaged by a government official not necessarily adept at that sort of thing, judging from the sloppy job and nonexistent bedside manner. Janet's hug is last, very Dorothy and the Scarecrow.

"Where are we going?" she asks, holding her ribs.

"Did anyone look at that?"

"I'm fine. Seriously, where are we going?"

"As a species or you and I in particular?" I counter.

She plants a kiss on me. "I hope I see you again one day, DJ."

I plan on watching her walk away, but the folks "in charge" have other plans. I am hoisted by my good arm by a sunglass-and-windbreaker-wearing agent over to a waiting helicopter. I want to point out it's evening but decide against it. "You're in this baby," he tells me.

I climb in and Ivan, Smack and Mercedes are already seated inside. Mercedes is looking at me ruefully, or so I tell myself, sitting alongside Smack, seemingly having watched my goodbye moment.

"I'm glad you're all right, man," I tell Smack. He looks over at me, sighs, doesn't know what to make of me. No one does, least of all me.

"How's the arm?"

"Jerking off's outta the question for a bit," Ivan interjects. "Shit. Sorry, Mercedes."

"It's cool."

"At least it's not self-inflicted, Ivan," I say. "Jesus. I can't believe I thought you were becoming a zombie all this time."

Our pilot cranes his neck, alternately flipping

switches, and watching another chopper take off. "Y'all strapped in?" We tell him yes in unison.

"I hate flying," Ivan says shortly after take off.

"Don't think about it," Mercedes suggests, rubbing the back of his hand softly.

"Or better yet," I interject. "Try this: Nam-myoho-renge-kyo."

We rise above the casino, up and over its highest floor, the floor dedicated to the high-rollers, the people who couldn't buy their way out of this, the floor empty and longing for the days when swollen businessmen filled them with girls a third their age, cocaine, and tips for the maids that they could retire on. It's a clear night and the stars have a new sparkle. So much so that both Ivan and Smack's obvious annoyance at my Buddhist suggestion doesn't even interfere with my acknowledgment of this; this along with the day's remaining clouds, like fresh snow in the night sky.

"So," the pilot bellows back to us, the *NYPD* on the back of his jacket somehow disconcerting. "You guys hear about that *Remember Connecticut* concert? They just added another performer."

www.ingramcontent.com/pod-product-compliance
Lightning Source LLC
Chambersburg PA
CBHW071210260626
47162CB00004B/1243